THE
DOOR
THAT LED TO
WHERE

THE
DOOR
THAT LED TO
WHERE

SALLY GARDNER

Delacorte Press

Text copyright © 2015 by Sally Gardner
Jacket art copyright © 2016 by Neil Swaab

All rights reserved. Published in the United States by Delacorte Press,
an imprint of Random House Children's Books, a division of
Penguin Random House LLC, New York. Originally published in
hardcover by Hot Key Books, London, in 2015.

Delacorte Press is a registered trademark and the colophon is a trademark
of Penguin Random House LLC.

Visit us on the Web! randomhouseteens.com

Educators and librarians, for a variety of teaching tools, visit us at
RHTeachersLibrarians.com

Library of Congress Cataloging-in-Publication Data
Names: Gardner, Sally, author.
Title: The door that led to where / Sally Gardner.
Description: New York : Delacorte Press, [2016] | Summary: When sixteen-
    year-old AJ Flynn finds a mysterious key at his new job at a London law
    firm, he and his scrappy friends begin a series of journeys to 1830 where
    they discover a crime only they can solve.
Identifiers: LCCN 2015034396 | ISBN 978-0-399-54997-7 (hardcover) |
    ISBN 978-0-399-54999-1 (ebook)
Subjects: | CYAC: Time travel—Fiction. | London (England)—Fiction. |
    Mystery and detective stories.
Classification: LCC PZ7.G179335 Do 2016 | DDC [Fic]—dc23

The text of this book is set in 10.5-point Berling.
Interior design by Ken Crossland

Printed in the United States of America
10 9 8 7 6 5 4 3 2 1
First American Edition

For my son, my sunshine,
Dominic Corry, with all my love

CHAPTER 1

"You will never amount to anything, AJ Flynn. Not with one GCSE."

Here she went again, drumming into him the heavy-metal sentence of failure. But today, a month after he'd received his disastrous GCSE results, his mum's rage seemed to have developed a purpose. This time her fury was accompanied by a culinary cacophony, as if the pots and pans were personally responsible.

"Do you know what you are?" she continued, slamming a cupboard door and clanking the frying pan down on the stove. The question was more a flying saucepan lid than anything requiring an answer. "Shall I tell you?"

AJ knew of no way to stop her.

"A waste of space, that's what you are. Sixteen years and what's to show for it? One bleeding GCSE."

AJ stood in the small kitchen of their three-bedroom flat while his mother peeled tough pink strips of bacon into the frying pan and let them fizzle in the fat. In such close proximity, AJ's only protection was to imagine her as the monster from the depths of despair, a red reptile with a poison tongue. Here it went, lashing out again. If you let it strike you it could cause serious damage.

"You've been nothing but trouble since the day you were born. Well, don't think that Frank is going to let you slouch round the flat doing nothing."

From the lounge came the voice of Frank.

"Jan," he shouted, "bring us a beer."

Frank and a marshmallow three-piece suite from Sofa World were the flat's latest acquisitions. The suite took up all the space the lounge had to offer, while Frank had taken over the flat. He was a huge, blancmange slug of a man who left a slimy trail of beer cans, bacon sarnies and spittled cigarette butts behind him.

"Tell him," Frank added helpfully from the depths of the marshmallow reclining armchair. "Tell him he can bugger off. What about that beer, Jan?"

AJ felt a flicker of hope. This might be the moment he could vaporize and disappear into the world outside. After that it was down five flights of stairs to where freedom awaited him in the comforting wheeze of London, the siren wail of calm. Sorted.

But instead of robotically doing what Frank demanded, his mum handed AJ a letter. It was addressed to Ms. J. Flynn and from a law firm, Baldwin Groat. AJ's heart sank.

"What's this?" he asked.

"What does it look like?"

"An official letter," said AJ. "But what's it got to do with me?"

"You can read, can't you?"

AJ read. Mr. Morton Black would like to see him tomorrow for a job interview.

"What kind of job?" asked AJ.

"I don't care," said Mum. "If it's cleaning the bogs, you'll bloody well take it."

"But how does he know about me?"

"I bloody well told him, didn't I."

AJ knew that more questions would not lead to more answers. The conversation would end with the reptile's famous saying: "Because I bloody well say so, that's why."

End of questions.

A woebegone wail came from Frank. "Jan—my beer—where is it?"

"Can't he get his own beer?" said AJ. "He needs a bit more exercise than just a workout on the remote control."

It was an unwise thing to suggest at the best of times. The beer destined for Frank hurtled towards AJ.

From the reptile-handling manual: In the event of attack, the best course of action is to run for it.

AJ made his exit as fast as he could, followed by the enraged red reptile, who, leaning over the metal-railed bannister, yelled down the stairs after him.

"You good-for-nothing little . . ."

Elsie, from three flats below, was already out on the landing looking up.

"Keep it down, Jan," she called.

"Shut up, you nosy old cow, and mind your own business."

The door to AJ's flat slammed shut. The noise vibrated through the whole building. If a full stop had a sound, AJ reckoned that was it.

"On one of her mad ones, then?" said Elsie. "Come in, love,

I've another book for you to take back to the library, if you wouldn't mind. And this time, bring me something with a bit of romance in it."

Elsie Tapper had been AJ's savior since he was old enough to walk down the stairs on his own. She had taken him in, even kept him for weekends when Jan wanted to have a break. AJ, in return, called her Auntie, as did his mates, Leon and Slim.

He liked her flat. It was like being in a time warp. The wallpaper was from the 1950s, and it had the original kitchen and parquet flooring. The hallway was lined with pictures of Elsie's daughter, Debbie, who now lived in Australia, and her son, Norris, who had disappeared years ago when he was twenty-three. What had happened to him was a mystery.

In a way, AJ had always known he filled the hole Norris had left and because of that he never asked about him. It would be, he thought, treading on a thin membrane of painful memories. AJ loved Elsie. He liked the fact that time and fashions had changed but everything around her stayed the same, ageless and safe.

"Is that right, then, about your exam results?" asked Auntie Elsie, taking him into her lounge.

Elsie's lounge still had its 1930s tiled fireplace, which made it feel cozy, just like AJ imagined home might be.

"Yes, I only passed English. A*, though."

"I would've thought you'd have got a lot more. Such a clever lad."

"Perhaps not clever in the right way," said AJ.

"What are you going to do now?"

"I've got a job interview."

He showed Elsie the letter. She turned on her lamp and put her glasses on the end of her nose.

"Nice writing paper," she said. She held up the letter to the light. "It has a watermark—expensive—with an embossed name. Must be a posh place, these chambers. What're you going to wear, love?"

It was something that AJ hadn't thought about.

"What I have on," he said.

"No, love, you can't go like that for a job interview. Not to a place with an embossed name and watermarked paper. You wouldn't stand a chance." She disappeared into her bedroom. "Come here, I need some help."

AJ stood on a chair and took an old, battered suitcase down from the top of the wardrobe. Elsie opened it with pride.

"A bit of a teddy boy in his youth, was my Jim. He loved his clothes."

The jacket was checked with a velvet collar and velvet pocket flaps. The waistcoat was bright red, the trousers too long. Elsie said the shirt, which was a kind of silvery gray, had shrunk a bit.

"Go on," said Elsie. "Try them on."

AJ stood looking at himself in the mirror. Only the crêpe-soled shoes and the shrunken shirt fitted; everything else was too big and made him look like a clown.

"I can't go dressed like this," he said.

"From where I'm standing it doesn't look like you have much option," said Elsie.

5

"Can I borrow the shoes and the shirt?"

"They're yours, love, if they'll help," said Elsie. "But what about a jacket?"

The next day, dressed in jeans, the gray shirt and the brothel creepers, minus a jacket, AJ set off for the job interview, his stomach doing the dance of death. Through his teenage years AJ had found a way of giving himself a boost of good luck when he needed it. He would search for signs—words in adverts would do; even a white feather in the road meant his guardian angel had him safe. Never, he thought, had he needed a sign more than he did that morning as he stood at the gates to Gray's Inn, watching all the fancy-pants ants with umbrellas and suits arrive for work. The address on the letter was 4 Raymond Buildings. It was a Georgian terrace built of mellow London brick, definitely not the kind of place that would have a job for him. His mum must be losing her marbles. He wondered if it wouldn't be best if he gave the whole thing a miss, headed back to Stoke Newington and spent the day in the library, lost in a book.

That was when he saw it, moving slowly down the road, stuck in a jam like the rest of the cars. A brand-new red Porsche. It was the number plate that gave AJ the courage he needed. It read 1 GCSE.

CHAPTER 2

"Mr. Morton Black will be with you shortly," said a young man in a shiny suit, showing AJ into a large, book-lined room that smelled of hoovered carpets.

It possessed an imposing desk with no one behind it or in front of it. AJ was left wondering if it was the desk that was interviewing him instead of Mr. Black. It looked more than capable of judging him and finding brothel creepers and a teddy-boy shirt wanting. The desk was a dinosaur of a thing bearing not even a computer to make a nod at the modern world, just an inkstand with clawed feet. On the wall behind the desk was an oil painting of a gentleman in a full-bottomed wig that hung in two forlorn curtains, framing a blotchy pink face. He could almost hear him say in a voice of brass and wind, "You will never amount to anything, AJ Flynn. Not with one GCSE."

What in all the dog's-dinner days had given his mum the crazy idea of writing to this law firm? He tried and failed to think what she might have said that would make even the cleaner agree to give him a job interview. He wondered if he was meant to sit in one of the chairs in front of the desk.

He could imagine it tipping him off the minute he tried, saying, "I only seat clients. Clients with well-padded bottoms and well-lined pockets."

AJ waited and waited, then, fearing his voice might have left him, said out loud, "'It would not be wonderful to meet a Megalosarurus, forty feet long or so, waddling like an elephantine lizard up Holborn Hill.'"

"*Bleak House*," boomed a voice. The collywobbles in AJ's stomach did a somersault as, from an unseen door in the bookcase, a gentleman appeared. "The everlasting quagmire of Jarndyce and Jarndyce," he said.

AJ stared into the face of a jolly-looking man with eyes that twinkled and a rubicund nose not dissimilar to the nose in the portrait. "Rate him, do you? Mr. Charles Dickens?" asked this apparition.

AJ wondered if his tongue had lost the power of speech. The best he could do was mumble, "He's the beat master."

"The what?"

"He pumps out the rhythm of rhyme, keeps a story ticking."

"Well, that's one way to describe it. 'My father's family name being Pirrip.'"

"*Great Expectations*."

"'Old Marley was as dead as a door-nail.'"

"*A Christmas Carol*."

"'It was the best of times, it was the worst of times,'" continued the man, "'it was the age of wisdom, it was the age of foolishness.'"

"*A Tale of Two Cities*," said AJ.

The apparition chuckled.

There was a knock on the door and a man in his late thirties entered the room. He had short-cut hair and a gaze that summed you up and kept the verdict to itself.

"I'm sorry, sir. I've no idea what Stephen was thinking. I'm supposed to be interviewing Ms. Flynn's son in my office."

"I take it then that you are Aiden Jobey," said the gentleman from the bookcase. AJ felt the carpet to be moving in a not-altogether-helpful way. "You are Aiden Jobey?"

AJ felt a momentary panic. There must have been a mix-up.

"I'm known as . . ." He stopped himself. Perhaps by claiming this new name that fitted his two initials he would at least sound like someone. "Yes," he said.

"Good. And my name is Groat." He held out a hand. AJ shook it. "And this is Morton Black, our senior clerk, whom we call Morton. If we take you on you will be working under him. Do you know, Morton," said Mr. Groat, sitting down behind his desk, "this young man has an exceptional knowledge of Dickens."

AJ hadn't a clue if that fact interested the senior clerk or not, for his face remained a perfect blank.

"I see from your mother's letter," Mr. Groat continued, "that you passed English with an A*. She writes of her great disappointment—spelled incorrectly—that you didn't do well in your other exams. Why didn't you do well, Aiden?"

AJ was battling to think straight. There was no mistake. This never-before-heard name, Aiden Jobey, belonged to him.

"I spent all my time in the library because school was noisy. I loved English. I loved history, but we only did the twentieth century."

Mr. Groat half closed his eyes so that only a slit of white could be seen. He looked like the prehistoric lizard.

"What do you know about the law?" he asked.

"Very little, but I want to learn," he said, cursing himself for not being better prepared.

Morton Black studied him. AJ felt as if the senior clerk was looking inside his head and didn't much like the decor.

"Do you cope well under pressure?" Morton Black asked him. "By that I mean in difficult circumstances?"

"I've coped with my mother for over sixteen years and that hasn't been easy."

Mr. Groat burst out laughing. "You're sixteen years old?"

"Seventeen next week. I'll do anything," said AJ. "I don't mind what it is, I just want to work."

Mr. Groat tapped his hand on the desk, which responded as if it were a bass drum. He stood up and looked out the window across Gray's Inn Gardens.

"You are obviously a bright young man," said Mr. Groat. "Wouldn't you agree, Morton?"

"Yes, sir. But I am somewhat intrigued to know how Aiden managed one A* GCSE and no more."

AJ, convinced now that the whole thing was hopeless, thought he had nothing to lose in telling the truth.

"I didn't much take to school. Or school didn't much take to me. They always wanted us to learn things that I had no interest in. There are so many books out there . . . about different times, amazing worlds, knowledge without limits. I didn't . . ."

AJ stopped. He was trembling, his knees wobbly. He hadn't

cared about getting a job at this law firm, not until now. Suddenly all he wanted was to work there.

Morton Black asked what else had he read in the library.

"Thomas Carlyle on the French Revolution." He had read that after *A Tale of Two Cities*. "And I loved *The History of the Decline and Fall of the Roman Empire*. It's the best piece of fantasy history I've ever read. Apart from Tolkien."

"What did you want to do when you left school?"

"Well, up to a few minutes ago I didn't have a clue," said AJ. "But now I would like to work here. I'm a quick learner."

On it went. AJ wondered if some of the questions were tricks to trip him up, because they came faster and snappier, almost too fast to think about. AJ was positive he had given the wrong answer to each one. Finally he was told to wait outside. He stood in the corridor and thought it was all over bar the shouting. He shouldn't have mentioned Tolkien in the same breath as *The Decline and Fall*. It sounded stupid.

He waited, watching the busyness of the chambers, and a wave of despair come over him. He was certain he'd blown it. The idea that he stood a chance of being employed here was off-the-wall crazy. His mum's words echoed in his head. "You don't get to wear a suit to work, not with one GCSE."

"Aiden." Morton Black stuck his head out of Mr. Groat's office. "Would you come back in?"

AJ had so successfully persuaded himself that he was unemployable that for a moment he couldn't work out what Mr. Groat was saying.

"We would like to offer you a three-month trial period as a baby clerk," he said.

"It's a glorified way of saying you will be an office boy," said Morton. "Your job will be to assist Stephen, the first clerk, and myself, maintaining the stock of stationery and chambers' brochures, updating the chambers' library, collecting and delivering documents."

"Will I be paid?" asked AJ, hearing the red reptile breathing down his neck.

"Most certainly," said Mr. Groat. "Not much to begin with, but if you prove yourself you will be put on a salary, and if you work hard, one day you might even become like Morton, a senior clerk, thinking he'll retire at fifty-three. You will prove yourself, won't you, Aiden?"

There it was again. That incredible name. Could it really belong to him?

"Yes, sir. I will do my best, my very best."

Had he heard them right? They were offering him a job, for real.

"Good. Welcome to Baldwin Groat, Aiden."

The minute Morton and AJ were out of Mr. Groat's office, Morton turned to him, not in an unpleasant manner, but firm, as if he meant business.

"You start on Monday, and I want to see you suited and booted. No brothel creepers, no cowboy shirt."

AJ nodded.

"Eight-thirty sharp, and I don't tolerate lateness."

AJ stood on the pavement staring up at 4 Raymond Buildings, still unable to take in what had just happened. He wondered if by going through the door that led to Baldwin Groat's chambers he had altered everything. He had gone in jobless, hopeless and nameless, and come out with a job, a glimmer of hope and a name he'd never heard before.

All his life his mum had made no bones about telling him that A and J were just initials, nothing more. Those two meaningless letters had been a problem at school. He had stood out when all he wanted was to fit in.

"It's not a proper name," his teacher had told him.

She had insisted he spelled it out: *A-J-A-Y*, until his mum had said with the subtlety of a cement mixer, "No, he's just an *A* and a *J*."

What she wouldn't tell the teacher was what those two stunted initials stood for, and she definitely wasn't going to tell AJ. By the time he reached secondary school he'd given up asking her. The question of his name belonged with numerous other unanswered questions, like who his father was, or even what had happened to his father. That much she eventually told him.

She had said, without a trace of emotion, "Dead."

AJ had assumed that the letter *J* must be the first letter of his father's surname. He'd imagined it to be something like Jones—certainly nothing as exotic as Jobey. He said it over and over again. Jobey. Aiden Jobey. It felt as if it was a password to a future. In Aiden Jobey there was space to grow. AJ had always felt like a dead end. As he arrived back in Stoke Newington the name was beginning to fit him, although the mystery of why he had never been told it before hung over him in a black cloud.

CHAPTER 3

It was a mild September day, that time of year when the seasons haven't yet made up their minds whether it's still summer or the beginning of autumn. While Clissold Park smelled of dried leaves and overheated grass that had long forgotten the color green, the chestnut trees braced themselves for the annual conker bashing. AJ was desperate to share the news of his job with someone other than his mum, whose reaction had been predictable to say the least.

"You can start paying for your board and keep," she said. "Don't think I'm a bleeding hotel."

He had thought about asking her for a loan for a suit, but he knew what she would say: "Do you think I'm made of money?" So he hadn't asked and he had a job and no suit.

It was a relief to escape the flat, to head off to the skate park. He hoped to find his two best friends, Slim and Leon. He could rely on them being there as long as the weather was fine, but today he found Slim alone, attached as always to his one and only possession, his skateboard.

Slim, with dark hair and brown eyes, was taller than AJ, more grown into himself.

"Where've you been?" he asked.

"I had a job interview."

"A job interview? That's impressive, bro," said Slim. "Where at?"

"A law firm," said AJ. "Called Baldwin Groat."

"You're joking, man. You mean a cube farm? Did you get the job?"

"Yeah, on trial. Office boy. The place doesn't exactly have cubicles, more huge rooms lined with books."

"Shit. What did you do to make that little miracle happen?"

"Nothing. Mum wrote a letter."

"That's heavy. What did she write? That she would do them over unless they gave you employment?"

"Something like that," said AJ, and changed the subject. "Why is Leon not here?"

"Wait a mo," said Slim. "How did your mum know about a toff place like that?"

"She had a job cleaning for them before I was born."

"Hold that picture, bro: so she knows these dudes, and after nearly seventeen years she's written to them and they've come over all fairy godmother and given you a job. Now, why doesn't that add up in my book?"

AJ didn't want to think about the whys of it or how Mr. Groat knew what his initials stood for.

"Leon," he said. "Where is he?"

"As my rap of the 'Electronic Jungle of Despair' goes, 'Life is shitty, times is gritty, Leon's been taken back into foster care.'"

"What happened?"

"His mum, being higher than a kite, thought she was a white

swan from a kiddies' book and flew off the balcony of their flat. Smack in her head, smack onto the pavement, smack into intensive care."

"When?" asked AJ.

"This morning."

AJ sat down next to Slim. There wasn't much to say. It was an old, scratched record they'd heard many times before. But the news of Leon's return into foster care took the shine off AJ's day.

Leon's mum was a drug addict. She loved her sons but couldn't look after them. The first time Leon and his little brother were taken into foster care was when their social worker discovered them eating cat food off the floor while the cat was on the table eating their breakfast. Leon's mum said she couldn't see the difference. The truth was she couldn't see anything. Leon's brother, Joel, was only eighteen months old then.

Their gran, a religious lady high up in the Church of the Celestial Coming, had taken Joel in. She said that Joel was definitely the child of her son, Amos, and still had the chance of being saved. But as far as Leon was concerned, she said he could never be Amos's son, being too pale in the skin. Hell's Highway already had Leon's name printed on the billboards. He was three when she'd had this helpful revelation, and because of it Leon had been in and out of care for the last thirteen years. After a lot of praying for guidance Gran had taken Joel home to Jamaica, leaving Leon battling to help his mum with her demons.

"Where have they taken Leon this time?" asked AJ.

"Back to the foster family in Muswell Hill. But they won't want him for long, as he's nearly seventeen."

As if reading AJ's thoughts, Slim said, "Nothing changes. We're all up against the white wall of hopelessness. My auntie couldn't care less about my exam results as long as I work at Uncle Jek's stall. The old geezer's only good for shouting out the bargains and being rude to the punters. He can't even count how many pints he's drunk. But wait a bit—if you have this job, don't you need to look the business?"

"Yeah. The trouble is I haven't any money to buy a suit. So as you say, life is shitty."

"What about your mum?"

"Are you a comedian?" asked AJ. "Roxy needs new trainers and the wheel fell off her scooter, so Mum is buying her a proper one from the bike shop." Roxy was AJ's half sister, the apple of Jan's eye. The word *no* never applied to her. "I thought about nicking a suit from Oxfam, but it wouldn't look good at the law firm if I was done for shoplifting."

Slim laughed. "Come on, bro. I've got an idea."

Unlike AJ, Slim had a family wardrobe stuffed full of relatives, distant, near, and a lot in between. He reckoned that if they stood hand in hand they would stretch the whole distance from Stokey to Dalston, maybe even as far as Shoreditch. AJ had never worked out where Slim fitted in this jammed wardrobe of unnamed relatives. It was one of the things AJ, Slim and Leon had in common: broken families.

They left the park and headed to Mr. Toker's laundry and dry cleaner's on Church Street. Inside, on the wall near the door, was a photo from the 1930s of five men playing golf outside a ramshackle laundrette. They weren't wearing trousers, just baggy knickers, and socks held up by garters. The sign read FREE GOLF WHILE WE PRESS YOUR SUIT.

"Yes?" said Mr. Toker, adding, "And no, I don't have a penny, if that's why you're here."

"No, bro!"

"Don't you *bro* me."

"Sorry. No, Uncle Şevket," said Slim. "AJ's got a job."

Mr. Toker studied AJ, not sure whether to take him seriously.

"Is this one of your high-flying, fancy stories?"

"No," said AJ. "I do have a job, but no suit, and without a suit I have no job."

"Do I look like a gentleman's outfitters?" said Mr. Toker. "Go away, the two of you, and stop wasting my time."

The other sign that AJ liked was smaller than the golf photo. It read ANYTHING NOT COLLECTED AFTER THREE MONTHS WILL BE SOLD.

AJ pointed to the sign.

"Please," he said. "I can pay for it on Friday. But if I don't have a suit for Monday, I'm stuffed."

Mr. Toker called to his wife. "Sarah. Do we have any suits that would fit this scallywag?"

AJ and Slim could see a large lady bending over a basket in the back room.

"No," she said. "Why would we?"

"There. You heard the oracle speak. Now bugger off."

18

"If you could just lend me one I will pay you back when I have my first paycheck," pleaded AJ.

Mr. Toker laughed. "Neither am I a pawnbroker." He sat down at the sewing machine behind the counter. "Go away."

"He will pay you, Uncle Şevket," said Slim. "I promise."

"How? Neither of you has a penny on you."

The sewing machine's click-clack agreed with its boss.

"Not a penny, not a pound," it seemed to say.

"I'll leave my skateboard here—it's worth good money," said Slim.

Mr. Toker and the sewing machine stopped. Mr. Toker looked up.

"You would do that for your friend? You're sure?"

"Yes," said Slim, handing over his skateboard. "It's worth way more than a forgotten suit."

Mr. Toker put the skateboard under the counter, went to the shop door and turned the sign to CLOSED.

"All right. A deal's a deal."

Slim looked a little shaken.

Mr. Toker began to call out AJ's measurements to his wife, who sighed as she looked through the rails of unclaimed suits. Finally she pulled out one in gray.

"Go to the back and try it on," she said. "And here—take this shirt."

Apart from being made for someone altogether taller, the suit fitted AJ perfectly. Without a word, Mr. Toker pinned up the trousers and the cuffs, then stood back, squinting.

"Where is this job of yours?" he asked.

"Baldwin Groat," said AJ. "In Gray's Inn."

"The suit will be ready tomorrow after three," said Mr. Toker. "Thirty pounds is the price to have the skateboard back."

"I owe you," said AJ to Slim.

"Big-time," said Slim. "That skateboard is . . . everything."

"I know," said AJ. "I won't let you down—promise, bro."

CHAPTER 4

On Monday AJ turned up for work in the suit and a pair of brogues two sizes too big that he'd found on top of a clothes bank. There was no polite introduction to the workings of Baldwin Groat. Morton, the senior clerk, told him that if he was to survive there he would need wit and intelligence. AJ found himself thrown in the deep end of the legal soup.

"We don't need more staff," Stephen, the first clerk, had complained. "We manage perfectly well."

"Aiden was taken on by Mr. Groat," said Morton. "Any complaints should be addressed to him as head of chambers."

Stephen was twenty-seven and had been at Baldwin Groat since he was eighteen. The son of one of the junior barristers, he had wanted to become a lawyer like his father but finding the examinations beyond him had gone for the option of being a clerk. Such was his position, and so long had he stayed in that position that he saw any new clerk as a threat. AJ was no exception. Stephen instantly took a dislike to him.

"Does Mr. Baldwin know about this new baby clerk?" he asked the senior clerk.

"Is that any business of yours, Stephen?" Morton snapped.

"No, but it's—"

"It's none of your business."

As far as AJ could make out from the junior barristers, the most dynamic of the QCs in the practice was Mr. Baldwin. He was abroad on a case and AJ had peeped inside his room. A photo of the eminent Queen's Counsel sat on the desk in a silver frame. AJ couldn't understand why he would want a picture of himself unless it was to remind him who he was. From the photo AJ decided that he was a man who took himself very seriously indeed, a man without a chin, and with a bottom lip much bigger than the top, which combined to squeeze themselves into a pout.

Mr. Groat, who had no photos of himself, or anyone else for that matter, was seen as something of an eccentric.

Whenever they were alone Stephen took delight in telling AJ exactly how short his career in the law firm would be.

"When Mr. Baldwin's back you'll be out on your butt," said Stephen. "One GCSE. You think Mr. Baldwin will stand for that? He only takes the brightest and the best. You can't say you quite fit the description."

AJ was used to bullies. They were to be found in every gang he had ever come across. He ignored Stephen.

"You don't need to charge about the place," Stephen would say. "You just get us more work."

Again AJ ignored him. He would rather be doing anything than standing there looking like a hatstand as Stephen did.

On the Friday of his first week, Morton called him into his office.

"You're for it," said Stephen helpfully. "I didn't think you'd last longer than a week. Never mind. You can put it down to work experience."

AJ stood in front of the senior clerk's desk. "You're a quiet one, Aiden," said Morton. "Do you like it here?"

The idea that he might like or dislike the job was a luxury of thought AJ hadn't allowed himself.

"Yes," he said.

"Have a good weekend."

His seventeenth birthday, hardly remembered, was quickly forgotten. That Saturday AJ was able to get Slim's skateboard back and they went in search of Leon. They reckoned the best place to find him would be the undercroft of the Southbank Centre. The three of them had been going there since they were eleven.

October had come in unseasonally warm, taking everyone by surprise. Half the inhabitants of London were slow-cooking in new winter clothes, while the other half were out to shimmer in the sunshine in shorts and skimpy dresses, doing their best to chase away the thought of autumn altogether.

It was a relief to find Leon, though he looked tired and thinner. His mum was still in a coma and he visited her whenever he could. His foster family meant well but thought that he shouldn't see her, that it wasn't good for his stability.

"I ain't going back there," said Leon. "I'd rather live rough than stay in that up-its-arse house. They eat brown rice and shit like that, full of what's good for you. They say that if I carry on living with Mum, I'll end up just like her. They understand nothing except what they read in the *Guardian*. I tell you, life is better in the *Sun*. At least the women have boobs. I haven't been going to college either."

Of the three of them, Leon had done the best in his exams and been accepted at sixth-form college.

"What're you going to do?" asked Slim.

"Move back home. Live there on my own. I'm not a kid."

"Live on what?" said AJ.

"That's where I thought you might help me out, bro."

Leon disappeared down the ramp.

"In the nineteenth century," AJ said to Slim, "we would've been considered men by now. Do you ever think that you were born in the wrong century? At the wrong time, to the wrong parents?"

"No, never. All I know is we all live in the Electronic Jungle of Despair."

On Monday, AJ noticed that no one in chambers slouched, nor did the junior barristers linger in the clerks' room. The day was wired tight.

AJ waited anxiously to be called into Mr. Baldwin's office. Stephen had a knowing look about him.

"I wouldn't make yourself too comfortable here," he said. "If Mr. Baldwin doesn't like you—well, that's that."

Charles Baldwin QC was a well-dressed man, a time fighter, someone who invested a lot of energy in staying young. A smug smile stuck firmly to his tight features.

"So you're Aiden Jobey," he said, greeting AJ with a pat on

the back. "Morton speaks highly of you. He thinks you could well make a good clerk. I knew your father, you know."

Had AJ heard correctly? This lawyer had known his father. Why hadn't Mum mentioned it? Surely it was important.

"And Janice, your mother," Mr. Baldwin continued. "I remember her well. She was a pretty little thing."

AJ wondered if Mr. Baldwin was muddling him up with someone else. It was hard to imagine that the red reptile was ever a pretty little thing. AJ was completely wrong-footed by this plastic cheerfulness. It was not what he had been expecting, and he was quite at a loss. How had his mum come to make such a huge impression on Mr. Groat and Mr. Baldwin that seventeen years down the line they still remembered her? It would have helped if the red reptile had been more talkative on the subject, but like so much of her past it belonged in the deep freeze of things unsaid.

"A black coffee, please. Thanks, Aiden," said Mr. Baldwin.

AJ was dismissed.

"Well?" said Stephen, who was waiting outside.

"He wants me to make him coffee."

"As soon as you can, Aiden," shouted Mr. Baldwin through the office door.

At the end of a week of making coffee for Mr. Baldwin, AJ found to his amazement he still had a job. Stephen was furious, almost green round the edges.

"Don't start thinking you're going to last here," he hissed, "because you're not."

What AJ had seen of Mr. Baldwin he hadn't much liked. He thought of him as two-faced. One face was all cultured charm, the other, fast fury, like a sports car in seventh gear. He didn't trust the eminent lawyer—neither could he work out why he was so interested in AJ's family.

"Where's your father now?" Mr. Baldwin asked one morning as AJ brought in his coffee.

"Dead, sir. I never knew him."

"Oh, sorry to hear that. I recall that he didn't have a will—I tried to convince him to write one. But I suppose he thought he had plenty of time. So do you have anything to remember him by?"

"Like what, sir?" asked AJ, feeling that he was missing something behind the question.

"Oh, I don't know," said Mr. Baldwin. "A memento, perhaps?"

"He left me nothing, sir," said AJ. "Not even a name."

Stephen looked as if he could willingly murder AJ for usurping his position, but Mr. Baldwin and his team soon became consumed by a forgery case and Stephen was once more indispensable.

Two weeks later, on a Monday morning, Morton found a note Mr. Baldwin had left for him, saying that he was taking a long weekend and would be back on Wednesday. Morton was not best pleased. Mr. Baldwin's mobile went straight to voice mail and he had left no other contact details. Even Stephen, who kept Mr. Baldwin's diary, was in the dark as to his whereabouts.

"Mr. Baldwin is very discreet about his private life," he said. "But he may have been going to a fancy-dress ball. I found this on his desk."

It was a receipt for the hire of a costume from Angel's in Shaftesbury Avenue.

"I'm not asking for gossip, Stephen, I'm asking if you know where he is."

"No, Morton, I don't."

"I just hope he has a good reason for dumping a hell of lot of work on Ms. Finch's plate," said Morton.

It was that week that AJ's life went from being ordinary to extraordinary in a way he could never have imagined, and like most unusual events, it started with no warning.

Morton asked AJ to sort out some files in the Museum. AJ hadn't seen any room in chambers that could be described as a museum, and by now he knew the place well enough. As you came through Baldwin Groat's door on the second floor, there was the reception desk with its huge, caring vase of flowers, comfy chairs for clients to sit on and a picture on the wall that showed a scene of eighteenth-century London. Next to reception was the clerk's room and Morton's office. Morton usually liked to keep his door open so that he could see who was coming and who was going. The first room down the corridor belonged to the junior barristers, Mr. Baldwin had the largest of the rooms by far and Mr. Groat's room was at the back, overlooking Gray's Inn Gardens. There was a small kitchen, loos and a photocopying room but nothing else, so what was Morton talking about?

The Museum turned out to be through a small door that AJ had thought was a broom cupboard. Here the archives were stored, file upon file of cases dating back decades. It was furnished with a solid table and a chair, but it was the collection of bizarre objects on the table that caught AJ's eye: a human skull, a compass, several bowler hats, pieces of jewelry and a box stuffed full of pocket watches and handkerchiefs. AJ could well imagine Fagin having once been a client of Baldwin Groat.

"What do I do with these things?" asked AJ.

"File them in boxes and mark them to the relative cases. It will take you the best part of a week. It's needed doing for ages."

One of the reasons that AJ had done so disastrously at school was simply the noise: the clatter in the classroom, the bells ringing, the stampede after lessons, the screaming children in the playground. There was enough noise at home. What he had longed for was silence. He had started skipping school to go to the local library. There, no one was allowed to speak; noise was banned. It was three months before he realized that with a library card he could take books home. Solemnly he read through the alphabet of children's literature. It was Mr. Montgomery, the senior librarian, who found AJ reading *Oliver Twist*, and with his help AJ discovered the rest of Mr. Dickens's work.

The Museum proved to be an education in itself—a library of criminal cases. AJ studied the ancient writing—legal mumbling that he didn't understand—but underneath were stories of real people, people like him and Leon and Slim. By the end of the day he had barely started.

On Wednesday Mr. Baldwin returned, looking pale. He came to see for himself how AJ was doing.

"Come across any old skeletons?" he said.

"No, sir," said AJ.

"If you do, bring them to me."

On Thursday AJ pulled a dusty file from the shelf. What was written on it made his stomach churn.

Jobey
1813

Jobey. The name that didn't belong to him but somehow did. He still hadn't dared raise the matter with his mother and didn't quite know why. He opened the file, hoping it might answer a few questions, but it contained only a map, hand-drawn on yellowed paper. Gray's Inn Road was clearly shown, and Mount Pleasant, just a few streets away—but what did Coldbath mean? And why was there an X just to the left of it? AJ took a photo of the map on his phone.

It was getting dark on Friday afternoon when he lifted the lid of the last battered cardboard box. Inside was a rusty iron key about ten centimeters long, the stem turned and decorated. The end that went into the lock had a zigzag line down its center. It belonged to a time when a key had more weight to it than it did today. This was a key you didn't lose.

A label was tied to the ring. Written on it in beautiful handwriting were the words

The property of A. Jobey, Esq.
2nd October, 1996

AJ blinked and looked at it again to make sure he had read the date right. It was the day he was born.

CHAPTER 5

It must be a mistake. The writing looked genuine enough: firm, slanted, in sepia ink. Maybe whoever had written the label had been in a hurry and got the date round the wrong way. He went to find the file he had come across the day before, the one marked Jobey. Perhaps he'd missed something. But it was not where he'd put it. Neither was it under the table, nor had it slipped down the back of the bookcase. The more he looked, the more certain he became that something was wrong.

He had worked hard that week and the table was cleared of all its bizarre items, each marked and filed to the relevant case. Only the key was left. It was dark outside now, the year closing down in the November night. AJ put the key in his pocket. Come Monday he would ask Morton if he knew why his name should be on the label and if he knew who had taken the file.

Everyone had gone home and the place was in darkness. AJ stood in the corridor, running his hand along the wall, unable to find the light switch. Each of the rooms was closed, as was the clerks' room, and he could barely see the reception desk. It must have been much later than he'd thought, for the only light there was came from the glow of the streetlamps. The building smelled of old documents, musty papers—not unpleasant, but a smell AJ hadn't noticed before, as if it was the same place but wasn't. Fear crept up on him. The chambers are haunted, that's it, he thought. They're ancient enough to be jam-packed full of ghosts, all of them miserable, all of them feeling the law had wronged them. The sooner he was out of there the better.

He made his way along the softly carpeted corridor, his outstretched hands guiding him. At Mr. Baldwin's door he realized he was not alone. He could hear voices coming from inside.

"What do you want from me?" Mr. Baldwin was saying, his usual rich, booming voice stuttering. "I'm a sick man—I need to go home."

Another voice hissed and spat the fat of unheard words.

AJ found no comfort in the familiar voice of Mr. Baldwin. Something was not right, and instinctively AJ knew he shouldn't be there.

He had started to creep back to the Museum when Mr. Baldwin said, "Are you threatening me, Ingleby? For God's sake, why would I? The boy doesn't even know about the door. Now let me go home."

AJ paused. He couldn't make out the words of Mr. Baldwin's companion, for they were as soft as shoeshine.

Then Mr. Baldwin said quite clearly, "Without the key, Jobey's Door can never be locked. You know that, I know that."

AJ slipped into the Museum, closed the door and held his breath. He waited until he heard the door to the chambers close. It was a heavy Georgian thing that had more noise to it than a door should. He gave it a moment or two. No one was there. This, then, was his chance to escape. On the landing he looked cautiously over the stair rail, then ran down the two flights of stairs and through the swing doors onto the pavement. To his surprise he found that he was in a fog unlike any he had ever encountered. It was so dense that his hand vanished when he held it before him. The fog whirled in the basements and through the railings; it gathered in pockets, and in it AJ saw ghosts from another time.

Elsie had often talked about the "pea soupers," as she called the notorious London fogs of her youth.

"So blooming thick that as a kiddiewink I thought they were made of all the buried people of the city come back to stretch their bones."

AJ could well see what Elsie meant. Thinking of her calmed him until he felt someone near him and an irrational terror overwhelmed him. He ran along beside the railings, using them to guide him to the gates of Gray's Inn.

He tugged at the gates desperately and only then remembered they were locked every night.

A voice, close by, hissed, "Mr. Jobey—is that you?"

"Let me out!" AJ shouted. "Let me out!"

Through the fog he felt a hand grab at his arm.

"I'll see you at Jobey's Door," said the voice.

"Get off me, you jerk," said AJ, and it was then that the gate suddenly opened and an old gentleman carrying a walking stick and a carrier bag full of books crashed into him. The bag broke and everything went flying.

"I'm sorry, I'm really sorry," said AJ. "I was . . ."

He bent down to pick up the walking stick and help gather the books. A white pigeon's feather fluttered from one of them. A good sign, thought AJ. He expected the man who had clutched at his sleeve to appear at any moment, but when AJ stood up he found the thick fog had disappeared, replaced by a mellow mist more suited to a London autumn, and there was not another soul to be seen, beyond the gentleman with the books.

"Are you all right?" said the old gentleman.

He owned a head of wild, white hair and a face dominated by a nose of magnificent proportions. AJ handed him back the walking stick, but without the carrier bag it was impossible for the gentleman to carry the books.

"Where do you live?" asked AJ.

"4 Raymond Buildings," said the gentleman. "Top floor."

AJ's heart sank. He didn't want to go back to the building he had just left, but the gentleman had what Elsie would call a gammy leg. There was nothing for it.

"My name is Edinger, Professor Edinger."

"Mine's AJ."

The professor lived under the sloping roof of the top-floor flat, in what had once been a children's nursery. Below the windows ran a faded frieze depicting bunny rabbits. AJ had never before seen such a room; not because of the rabbits but because of the huge collection of books. There were books everywhere. Books propping up tables, books supporting shelves, books piled precariously on top of one another. On an old table sat a lopsided candelabra with half-melted candles, and on one wall hung a panorama of London dated 1642. Time here had not stood still; rather it had fallen backwards. He put the books on the table, causing a cloud of dust to rise.

"Sherry?" said the professor, reaching for a decanter.

AJ had never tried sherry.

"Why not?" he said.

The glasses were none too clean.

"They belonged to Napoleon," said the gentleman. The biscuits he offered looked as if they might have belonged to Napoleon too. They had a greenish tinge to them.

"No thanks," said AJ.

The sherry had at least stopped AJ's heart beating bass and drum.

"How is AJ spelled? Two *A*s and a *Y*?"

"No, just the initials. Short for Aiden Jobey. Or so I'm told."

"Very interesting," said the professor. "Very interesting."

AJ was mesmerized by the clutter in the room. On a small table propped up by books stood a rigged wooden galleon. It looked older than anything AJ had ever seen, as if it belonged in a museum.

"What's that?" he asked.

"Oh, it's a model of one of the ships of the Armada."

"Is that for real?" asked AJ. "Hell, this place is like an antiques shop."

"I suppose it is."

"And all these books—do you read them?"

"Yes. Do you read?" asked the professor.

"I love reading," said AJ, bending his head to have a better look at the spine of a book whose cover was so old it resembled wood. The professor passed it to him.

AJ opened it. "'*The Trial of Charles I*'," he read. "This was published in 1648."

It smelled of another time.

"You work for Mr. Groat, don't you?" said the professor, helping himself and AJ to another glass. Slightly light-headed, AJ saw that the professor's jacket was patched in places, the cardigan he wore under it was buttoned up wrong and his trousers bunched at the ankles.

"What happened out there?" asked the professor as if he was certain something had happened to AJ.

AJ told him about the fog and the voice, keeping his eye on the professor all the while, looking for traces of disbelief. There were none. AJ didn't mention the key nor the conversation he'd overheard, although he had a sickening feeling that it was about him.

As he was leaving the professor said, "I look forward to seeing you again, young man." He opened the door. "Just pop up, anytime."

Only as the door was closing did AJ catch his last words.

"Best you keep that key to yourself."

CHAPTER 6

The second AJ stepped into the stairwell at Bodman House that night, he knew there was trouble. He could hear plates smashing and his mum shouting. When he reached the second floor, Vera from the flat opposite Elsie's was on the landing.

"If she doesn't put a sock in it I'll do it for her."

AJ climbed the flights of concrete stairs dreading what would greet him.

"Oh, look what the cat's brought in," shouted his mum.

She was surrounded by broken crockery. The muffled sound of sobbing came from Roxy's room.

"What's going on?" asked AJ.

"What does it look like?" she said and pushed past him. "Frank!" she screeched.

Frank came out of the bedroom carrying a duffel. He looked done in; his usually grayish complexion had taken on an unhealthy, reddish glow.

"I'm not staying here. I've had enough," he said.

There was more action in Frank than AJ had seen since the day he and the marshmallow three-piece suite had moved in. There was not much room in the hall, and Frank took up most of it. The red reptile grabbed the handle of the duffel.

"Don't think you can run out on me without paying the rent," she said, trying to pull the bag off Frank.

A tug of war ensued, which didn't last long, as the bag's handle snapped, along with Frank's patience.

"Get off me, you old cow," he said, and slapped Jan hard.

She went at Frank, fists flying.

"Just quit it, Mum," said AJ.

Frank turned on AJ and the first blow caught his left eye. AJ ducked the rest as best as he could until Frank had him pinned flat on the marshmallow sofa in the lounge. It took AJ a moment to work out what Frank was shouting.

"It's kids that are the bleeding trouble. Never wanted them— not hers, not mine . . ."

"I never bleeding well wanted *him*—that's for sure," screamed Jan.

AJ thought about the straw that broke the camel's back: how much straw that camel had to carry before it realized it was too much. Too long he had put up with the crazy-paving pattern of violence. Seventeen years. Too long, far too long. He freed himself and landed such a punch on Frank's face that he fell, sprawled flat on his back, a beer-filled belch spilling from him.

"What have you done to him?" Jan shouted, leaning over Frank's prostrate body.

There was a moment of silence, that moment before the next record plays on the turntable.

"Frank, baby, are you all right?" sobbed the red reptile. "I'm sorry, cherry pie."

"Where're you going?" said Roxy, coming out of her bedroom. AJ was opening the front door.

"Don't worry," he said. "I won't be coming back."

He ran down the stairs, only vaguely noticing Elsie and Vera. Elsie called after him and Mrs. Perkins from the bottom flat said she'd rung the police.

"Someone could be murdered up there."

"Yeah, me," said AJ, and slammed the outside door.

He was so angry there was no way he could stop moving. It felt as if sparks of fire were flying off him, such was his frustration with his family, with all the crap that was his life. Fireworks exploded in the sky, sparks of gunpowder as red as his rage.

He squeezed through the gap in the fence next to the locked park gates and was drawn to the clatter of wheels and the sound of a skateboard as it hit the ground. AJ sat on a bench, not saying a word, watching Leon flip and olly down the bank.

"Safe, man," said Leon after a while, and handed AJ his skateboard.

AJ was nowhere near as good a skateboarder as Leon and Slim, but it was a release just to be on the board, to feel his body twist and turn, his breath coming deep and fiery.

The police were at Bodman House when they passed it. Leon lived two blocks away.

"What happened, bro?" he asked as he put the key in his door.

"Mum and Frank," said AJ.

"Damn," said Leon.

The flat Leon lived in with his mum could at best be described as raw. The place stank of mold, weed and cat's piss. The carpets almost moved without you walking on them. For all that, it was a darn sight more cozy that night than AJ's flat. They watched *Night of the Living Dead*, smoking weed, neither of them saying much. AJ fell asleep on the sofa.

At lunchtime the next day Slim turned up with pizza and Cokes.

"What went down at your manor last night, dude?" he asked AJ, who was in the kitchen trying to find a clean mug.

"Nothing much," he said, turning round.

"Wowzer," said Slim. "That is one impressive bruise."

AJ glanced at his black eye in the mirror. It wasn't good.

"I can't go to work like this."

Leon and Slim studied him.

"I don't know. The girls will love it," said Slim.

"Shut it," said AJ.

By Sunday evening it had been decided that AJ would stay at Leon's, at least until his mum came home. He'd pay Leon some rent—a bit more dosh would come in handy. AJ popped round to Elsie's to ask if he could use her washing machine.

"That looks bad, love," she said. "Hold on a mo." She went to her bathroom and came back with a tube of arnica. "When Debbie visited me from Australia, she brought this. Said it was good for everything."

AJ didn't like to say that it was so long since her daughter had visited that it might not work anymore. Nevertheless, he allowed Elsie to put the cream on his face, and the touch of her paper-soft skin made him feel better.

"What happened with the police?" he asked.

"I think they cautioned Frank. Jan said it was a 'misunderstanding.' There you go, love, nothing changes."

Monday came too soon, too bright. On his way to work, AJ felt the key in his pocket. The sharp, cold iron brought back the overheard conversation and the stranger's words. *I will see you at Jobey's Door.*

He shuddered at the thought. He knew what he was going to do. Give the key to Morton. And he wasn't going to ask about the Jobey file. Life was already complicated enough.

CHAPTER 7

When AJ was small he had seen letter boxes as metal mouths waiting to trap him; keyholes were eyes watching him. Still to that day, he felt a front door told you more about the inside of a house than anyone needed to know. Finding Baldwin Groat's door wide open that morning, he thought the chambers felt naked, vulnerable.

Morton was already attached to his phone.

"I'm trying to find out where Mr. Baldwin is. No, he's not in chambers. If he was I wouldn't be calling. Neither is he at the Old Bailey." He put down the phone. "Mr. Jobey," he said. He paused and took in AJ's black eye before continuing. "Stephen is off sick—you will be assisting Louise Finch."

Louise Finch was a barrister, a tall, elegant woman, and AJ, with a young connoisseur's eye for the ladies, would have described her as fit. Weighed down by briefs, wig and gown, they piled into a taxi and set off to the Old Bailey.

Ms. Finch looked intently at her iPad while AJ looked out the window and thought of the thousands and thousands of doors out there—maybe millions—each one with its own lock; of all the keys that guaranteed entry into homes, businesses, shops—each with an address and every address known to the key's owner. Here he was with an ancient piece of ironmongery, with a named door to call its own, that left an orange mark on his hand. The only thing he didn't have was the address. All weekend he had thought about the key. The more he thought, the more the key itched at him, for it gradually began to occur to AJ that it might unlock a door at the place shown on the map that he'd photographed in the Museum. He took out his mobile and studied the image, blew up the spot marked X as big as it would go. Curiosity nibbled the edge of his resolve to be rid of the thing.

It was a truth, he knew, that a mystery was almost irresistible. Take Bluebeard's wives, he thought. Bluebeard gave them the keys to the castle to look after while he was gone, told them they could open any room but one—and look what they did. They just couldn't resist it. He put his hand in his pocket, almost expecting to feel the key sticky with blood. A vision developed before him of this unknown Ingleby waiting in the shadows, a man with a blue beard.

"This is a forgery case," said Ms. Finch.

AJ jumped.

"I didn't mean to interrupt your daydreaming, Aiden, but I thought you might be interested in a little background to the case."

"Yes," said AJ. "I am."

"Our client, David Purcell, is an antiques dealer."

"What sort of antiques?" asked AJ.

"He specializes in rare snuffboxes, pocket watches and miniatures from the late seventeenth to early nineteenth centuries."

"Is there a big demand for that sort of thing?"

"Yes. Two years ago an eighteenth-century porcelain snuffbox made for King Augustus III of Poland was sold for 1.4 million dollars at auction in New York. Let's just say that our client deals with the top end of snuffboxes."

"You know 'snuff' means 'dead'?" said AJ helpfully. "As in, 'he snuffed it.' "

"Thank you," said Ms. Finch with a smile.

AJ had never imagined walking into the Old Bailey, let alone on the right side of the law. Yet here he was, sitting on a bench outside the robing room, waiting for a barrister.

"Now, Aiden," said Ms. Finch as she came out of the robing room, "the procedure is that you follow me into court and stay at the back in case I need something."

It was a day for firsts. AJ hadn't been sure what Court Number Two of the Old Bailey might look like. It definitely wasn't like any of the court rooms that you see on TV dramas—it was much more dignified: paneled walls, with a long bench in front of a row of leather-seated thrones, carved in oak.

The man in the dock, their client, was dressed in a snappy suit that was cut to impress, but without a tie the suit looked insulted. Mr. Purcell sat impassively in the dock with his head up, as if an unpleasant smell was wafting from the cells below.

"Order, order. Will the court rise for His Lordship," said the usher.

Everyone stood as an impressive judge in a red gown and wig entered and sat down. The court waited for the serious matter of the day to begin.

The first witness for the defense was a Mr. Paggs.

"Mr. Paggs," said Ms. Finch, "your expertise is in antique snuffboxes?"

"Yes."

"Please look at the snuffbox shown in photograph 401 in the evidence."

The jury shuffled through the documents to the right page.

"You have examined this snuffbox. Would you say that it is a fake?"

"No," said Mr. Paggs. "It's a puzzle."

"In what way?"

"Well, the case is in mint condition and the snuffbox looks as if it was made thirty years ago, but it wasn't. All the materials used are authentic, and there is no doubt that the artist is van Draydon, whose work in gold and miniature enamel painting is highly prized."

"Mr. Paggs, are you saying that it is a fake or an original?"

"I would stake my reputation on it being an original. We have had it X-rayed, and the processes involved in making an enamel snuffbox such as this no longer exist."

"And if this is an original, as my client claims, how much is it worth?"

"One and a half million—and that is a conservative assessment."

"Is it your professional opinion," said Ms. Finch, "that none of the items you have examined for this case are fake?"

"Most definitely. I have never seen such beautifully preserved antiques in all of my forty years in the business. It's as if they've been handed to us through a loophole in time."

There was a ripple of laughter.

The usher brought in a note and, bowing to the judge, gave it to Ms. Finch. She read it, then asked the judge if she might approach the bench. Whispering became chattering, and it grew louder and louder until the judge shouted, "Order, order. This case is to be adjourned for the rest of the day. I will see the counsels in my rooms."

AJ waited at the side of the courtroom while everyone else filed out. When they'd left, AJ went up to Ms. Finch. She was rereading the note that had brought the proceedings to such a sudden halt.

"What's happened?" he asked.

Ms. Finch said quietly, "Mr. Baldwin was taken into hospital on Friday night with suspected poisoning. He's in intensive care."

CHAPTER 8

At four o'clock AJ was sent home. He sat on the top of the 38 bus, his mind tumbling. He was a thousand miles from calm, and everywhere he didn't want to be. He had told Ms. Finch that he had worked late on Friday evening, sorting out the files in the Museum, and she had asked him casually if he had seen or heard anything strange. The words had lined up on the tip of his tongue to tell her about the man called Ingleby and even about Jobey's Door and the key with his name and date of birth on it. As luck went, he had been saved by the bell of her mobile phone, and he quickly swallowed the information deep into him. She didn't look as if she was expecting an answer.

It wasn't rational, but he felt guilty, as if in some way he was responsible for Mr. Baldwin having been poisoned. AJ had been responsible for everything bad since the day he was born. He told himself that the last thing he could let happen was to lose his job. Better by far to keep quiet. Anyway, who would believe him? AJ felt that his world had gone spinning off its axis.

It was at Mount Pleasant that he spied the professor with

his lopsided walk, his stick in his hand. AJ jumped off the bus and sprinted after him.

"Wait!" he called. "Professor Edinger, wait!"

The professor stopped.

"Ah, here you are, AJ," he said as if he had been expecting him. "How very good to see you again. Are you hungry?" The professor didn't wait for an answer, and AJ, who hadn't eaten at all that day, realized he was starving. "I always find that when one hasn't eaten, life feels decidedly perilous."

He lead AJ to a café on Rosebury Avenue.

"What would you like?" he said when they'd sat down.

AJ felt the miserable collection of coins in his pocket.

"Tea would be good."

The professor ordered sausages and mash for them both.

"On me," he said.

They ate in silence. Mouthful by mouthful AJ began to find his feet again.

"You still have the key?" said the professor.

"How do you know about the key?"

"Just a guess. Baldwin never found it, then?"

"Why was he looking for it?"

"Another cup, AJ?"

"I don't understand what's going on. I don't want the key." He took it out of his pocket and put it on the table. "I don't need any more trouble."

"May I?" asked the professor. He picked it up and looked at the label.

"Second of October nineteen-ninety-six. Your date of birth."

AJ nodded.

"Do you know where to find the door that it belongs to?"

"I have an idea. Look, this is all crazy, and I'm miles from safe. Tomorrow I'll have to tell the police what I saw—and what I heard."

"No," said the professor. "No. I would appreciate it if you didn't do that—not right away. The key has your name on it—surely it's at least worth investigating?"

AJ leaned forward. "Look, I could be in deep shit here. I could lose my job. This is not a game."

"No, far from it, AJ. It is a very weighty matter indeed, and one that I am not sure you are up to, which is a pity."

"What do you mean?"

"You know the story of Jack and the Beanstalk? His mother sends Jack to market with a cow. The boy has not had the best start in life. He sells the cow for three beans. His mother is furious and throws the beans out the window. The next day a giant beanstalk has grown there. Now, this is the interesting part: Jack has curiosity, he has courage. He is brave enough to take a chance and climb the beanstalk. And by doing so he changes his future."

"So what?" said AJ.

The professor put a gold pocket watch on the table and opened it. Inside was a painted scene of a house and garden. It was exquisite.

"How old would you say this is?"

"I don't know. It looks brand-new."

"Precisely. It is new—about forty years old. But it was in fact made in 1790." He put the watch back in his pocket. "I have made an extensive study of the phenomena of portals to other times."

AJ stood up.

"Thanks for the meal, but this is all way too weird for me."

"Wait," said the professor. "You say you know the location of the door that the key belongs to?"

"I worked it out. I found a map in a file marked *Jobey* and I took a photo of it on my phone. It's the waste ground at the side of the Mount Pleasant sorting office. It's used as a car park."

"Go there. Look for a lintel in an old wall—there is a dead buddleia root above it. You don't have to unlock the door. Shall I meet you back here . . . let's say, twenty-four hours from now? Then perhaps you will be able to answer the riddle of my pocket watch."

AJ felt unreasonably cross as he walked back towards the bus stop. The professor definitely had several screws missing from his toolbox. Who did he think he was? A deranged time lord? He shoved his hands in his pockets and felt the key.

"Beanstalks," he muttered. "Off his bloody rocker."

Tomorrow he would tell Morton all he knew. Then he would tell the Old Bill how he had heard Baldwin with someone else in his chamber, and about the voice in the fog. That was the only way to swim back to the shore of normality.

But AJ didn't catch the bus. Not the first one, nor the second. Instead, in the gloom of a darkening Monday afternoon, he made his way towards the car park in Mount Pleasant.

CHAPTER 9

It occurred to AJ as he climbed over the wall at Phoenix Place into the deserted car park that it was nearly always dark in horror films when perfectly sane people decided to do insane things. The waste ground at the side of Mount Pleasant sorting office looked terminally spooky. The old, jagged brick walls cast long shadows on the tarmac. His mind's eye saw white-faced zombies pushing through solid bricks, creeping out of grooves and cracks. What it couldn't see was a door. Best to leave, he thought. One other thing he knew about horror movies was this: even when the violin screeched out a warning to the actors that going alone into an empty car park where the zombies lived was a stupid idea, they never listened.

"Stop it," he said to himself, his mind churning.

He looked again at the photo of the map on his mobile. Phoenix Place wasn't marked on it, but as he turned towards the sorting office he saw the wall the professor had described to him. The shrub, no more than a dead root, appeared in the shadows as a devil's head with antlers. AJ was certain that at any moment it was going to speak.

He had spooked himself out of all rational thought. The only comfort was the feel of the concrete solid beneath his feet. Just when he believed he was mastering his fear of zombies, everything took a turn for the worse. A fog began to seep up through the cracks in the ground.

"This is well out of order," he said aloud.

He felt genuine fear rush through him. The fog was now all-encompassing, as thick as the one outside Raymond Buildings. He tried and failed to get his bearings. Panic was about to swamp him when the fog cleared and there it was: the door. How had he not seen it before? It wasn't the kind of door you could miss. A red door, set into the wall, framed by two wooden columns. Above it a stone face looked down at him in a not-altogether-welcoming manner. The sight of the face alone gave AJ the heebie-jeebies. He turned to walk away then caught sight of the door knocker—cast iron, molded in the shape of a man's hand. Carved into the door was the name JOBEY.

AJ took the key from his pocket, then remembered that the professor had said that the door wasn't locked. Trembling, he tried to push it open. It was heavy and had been so neglected that its hinges seemed to have seized up. Taking a deep breath and listening to the tribal drums of fear beating in his body, he leaned on it with all his weight. Quite suddenly it swung open and AJ found himself staring into a wood-paneled hall. It took a moment for his eyes to adjust to the morose darkness of his surroundings. The dust that lay thick on the floor was evidence that few people walked there. It smelled of damp mustiness, wax candles and coal smoke. More than the dust, more than the smell, the complete stillness, the absence of the never-ending hum of the city, made him aware that he had stepped over an unknown threshold. He waited, his heart drumming to a hip-hop beat, for the sounds of the London he knew to rush in upon him. He waited and there was nothing, just the patient tick-tock of a clock measuring a different time. Was it possible that the professor was right?

He nearly jumped out of his skin when the front door slammed shut behind him. A candle appeared on the stairs and gradually came closer.

"Is that you, Mr. Jobey?" called a voice from behind the candle.

The light danced in danger of extinction. When it rekindled AJ saw a well-built man, a long, dark coat softening his bulk; on his head was a battered velvet hat; a woolen muffler was wrapped several times round his neck. His eyes were mole-black and his nose sharply chiseled. A dust-filled cloud followed him as his coat swept the stairs. His mittened hand held the candle close to AJ's face.

"Mr. Jobey," he declared. "I have been eager to make your acquaintance, sir."

Perhaps, thought AJ, all this was the result of some crazy drug he didn't know he'd taken.

"How do you know who I am?"

"I have long been expecting you." From his pocket he drew a silver watch on a faded ribbon and clicked it open. "Come on, Mr. Jobey," said the man. "The clocks are ticking."

The man and the candle strode back up the stairs.

Wherever he was, the world AJ knew had just been swallowed up by a different reality. In the meager light of the one candle, he could see that chunks of plaster had fallen off the walls and parts of the cornice had crashed onto the stone floor of the hall. The banisters wobbled as AJ climbed the stairs, and he wondered if the whole house wasn't on the verge of collapse.

They came to a landing with three grand doors leading off it, and the man with the candle opened the one on the right. It was hard to make out the room's proportions for it was so dimly lit. What light there was came from the large, elaborate fireplace, where, in the grate, an apology of a fire struggled to make a little heat from a few coals. An unmade bed stood to one side; on the other was an armchair that had taken umbrage at the cold and placed its animal feet in the grate, so that it sat as near the embers as it could without becoming a part of them. AJ noticed what he supposed to be a stuffed magpie on a perch, and he jumped when the bird put its head to one side and studied him with a glint in its ebony eye.

"This is His Honor," said the man, pointing at the magpie. "So best you mind your Ps and Qs. There is nothing that His Honor doesn't know."

A door on the other side of the room opened, and in came a woman dressed in black, a calamity of a bonnet on her head and her clothes looking more fallen to pieces than those of the man who had brought him up here.

"Mother," said the man, "I told you to keep the door shut. If you let one of those cats of yours up here I will have its guts for garters."

"It's a sin, it is," the woman mumbled into the light, "to let a bird come between a mother and her son."

"It is a sin for a mother to keep eighteen cats when she knows that His Honor is in perilous danger by her so doing."

"Twenty-two," said his mother. "The Queen of Sheba had her kittens this morning."

"So we are stuck betwixt and between. I rest my case, Your Honor."

The magpie squawked in agreement. "A most discerning bird, a most intelligent *Pica pica*."

"Will you be wanting your gruel tonight?" said the woman.

"No, not tonight. I will be out."

"Out?"

"Yes. We have a visitor." Only then did the woman seem to notice AJ. "Mother, would you be so kind as to take him to the closet so that he might change into more appropriate garments?"

AJ followed her to a small room where clothes were laid out on a chair.

He dressed as if in a dream. Trousers, shirt, waistcoat and jacket—all felt soft and luxurious, and curiously warm. Finally he tried on a top hat and found that, like everything else, including the boots, it fitted.

"Come, the hour is late," said the man.

A sense of relief washed over AJ as they descended the stairs. There was the front door. For the first time he could see there was another stone face peering down at him with a gaze as unfriendly as its twin on the outside. His nameless host pushed the door open, and AJ found that the London he knew had vanished.

"Where am I?" he asked.

"Clerkenwell." The man laughed. "Can't you smell the sweet

54

waters of the Fleet River? And there, looming over us, is the monster that is Coldbath Fields Prison."

AJ was lost in a city he knew like the back of his hand. It was the same place but completely transformed. He tried to make sense of the impossible and failed. He clung to the one thing all humans cling to when everything has gone bottoms up—a name.

"What's your name?" he asked.

In the flicker of a streetlight he saw his companion smile.

"Why, my name is Ingleby."

CHAPTER 10

Ingleby walked on ahead. There was little choice but to follow him, though AJ's street wisdom told him that whatever century he was in it was unwise to accompany a man who was most probably a poisoner. If this had been the Clerkenwell AJ knew, where the road to Islington was tarmacked, not cobbled, where there were proper pavements, where there was a London bus, he would have jumped on it and gone home. But he wasn't even sure which direction home might be.

Ingleby stopped abruptly.

"Mr. Jobey, can you walk a bit faster? We have an appointment."

"Appointment for what?" said AJ, jumping back to avoid being covered in mud by a passing horse-drawn cab.

"If you keep dawdling and staring we will never be done with the business of the night," said Ingleby, taking hold of AJ's coat sleeve.

"Do you know Mr. Baldwin?" said AJ, playing the innocent. "He's been poisoned."

"That doesn't surprise me in the slightest, Mr. Jobey," said Ingleby. "There are some in this city—and in yours—who

would willingly pepper his dish. A greedy man, Mr. Jobey, has many enemies. I am not saying that I would not poison him; I'm not saying that I could not; I am only saying that I did not."

"You mean he—Charles Baldwin, QC—comes here?" said AJ. He was amazed to find himself in this past world, let alone to learn that his boss had been there before him. Still reeling from the news, AJ at first didn't notice a band of men come marching towards them in a drunken military order of sorts, colors flying, swords drawn. They marched to the beat of a kettle drum. One handed AJ a leaflet.

"Hockley?" he said, reading it.

"Bear-baiting, is that it?" said Ingleby with interest.

"Yes," said AJ, screwing up the leaflet and stuffing it in his pocket.

"Not to your taste, bear-baiting?" said Ingleby, laughing. "You can't use the future, Mr. Jobey, to wash clean the past."

At Chancery Lane they came to the gate to Gray's Inn. From a ramshackle shed that AJ had never seen before came a gatekeeper, pulling his muffler tight. He nodded to Ingleby, who walked on until the gatekeeper called him back.

"Haven't you forgotten something?" he said. "A man in my position needs to keep his strength up on a cold night like this."

"You are a rogue."

"Then I'm in good company, Mr. Ingleby," said the gatekeeper. He weighed the coins that Ingleby put in his hand. "How does your magpie do?"

"His Honor? Middling to fair. Middling to fair, now you've robbed him of his supper."

In the gaslight, Raymond Buildings looked newly built, more upright. Time hadn't burrowed into it. At number four, the name in gold writing on the door read GROAT STONE. Inside, new sandstone stairs, bare of the institutional carpet AJ trod every day, led up to one thing he could place in his time— the black gloss door. Even that had yet to acquire the years of repainting. The layout of the chambers was completely different. This, thought AJ, is what it must have originally looked like. In the outer office were clerks' tall desks and a small fireplace. Through the glass panes of another door AJ could see an inner office. Here was a large fireplace with a carnival of a blaze in the grate, and behind a majestic desk sat a stern, straight-backed gentleman with glasses on his head and glasses on his nose. In the flickering candlelight he appeared to have four eyes instead of two. His face, drained of all color, glowed bone-white.

Ingleby opened the glass-paned door.

"This is young Mr. Jobey, Mr. Stone."

All four eyes looked up to examine AJ.

"Here is snuff enough to tickle the nose of even the strongest resistance," said Mr. Stone. "You, sir, are a very mirror in which your father's face is reflected. And if any querulous soul is in doubt of your paternity, then the proof is the charm you have upon you."

AJ realized that far from feeling terrified—an emotion the situation surely demanded—he was positively excited. If this was real, and so far there had been nothing to prove it wasn't, then he was in one of the most extraordinary situations that any young man could find himself. This was his beanstalk in the gutter of time.

Mr. Stone was writing in a large book that lay open on his desk. Methodically he changed over his metal-framed glasses so that the pair from the top of his head found themselves on his nose and the pair on his nose found themselves on the top of his head. He put down his pen, closed the book, stood and went to the fireplace. From a jar he took a clay pipe and lit it.

"You are wondering, Mr. Jobey, about the door."

"Yes, sir."

"Do you know the rhyme about the magpie?

"No."

Mr. Stone took the pipe from his mouth.

> *"One for sorrow,*
> *Two for luck;*
> *Three for a wedding,*
> *Four for death;*
> *Five for silver,*
> *Six for gold;*
> *Seven for a secret,*
> *Not to be told—*

I will tell you the secret that is not to be told. Old Jobey, your grandfather, possessed a door to an unimaginable future. It had never been opened in living memory. Years ago it was believed by those who knew the door existed that by the twentieth century the world would have been destroyed. That was until in

1809, when Old Jobey, whose fortunes were dwindling, decided to look for himself. He took no notice of my warnings—far from it. I told him I feared he could be walking into the abyss. He was a stubborn man—he never listened to advice. He went through the door and discovered he could profit handsomely by trade with the future. Not being a young man, he took a partner, a Mr. Samuel Dalton, and it was then that two greedy men started to break every rule."

"There are rules?"

"Every game has its rules, Mr. Jobey," said Mr. Stone. "And it is a rule of time travel that you do not do business with the future. It is forbidden."

"Who by?" asked AJ.

"By gravity, by the laws of physics. The future has, by its very nature, to remain unwritten, always to be a blank page. When your grandfather handed the key to your father, Lucas, it was already too late. His fate and the fate of his family were sealed. And there lies the sorrow."

"What about my father?" said AJ. "Is he still alive?"

"Three for a wedding, four for death. Your father was murdered. The mystery of who murdered the Jobey family remains, as far as I'm concerned, unsolved. An innocent girl was sent to the gallows for it, and the door has stayed unlocked ever since. We were only lately informed of your existence."

"Who by?" asked AJ. "By Mr. Baldwin?"

"No, not Charles Baldwin," he said with distaste. He carried on. "According to Old Jobey's will, the house in Clerkenwell, with all its goods and chattels, is to be inherited by the first-born Jobey of each generation. That first-born, sir, is you."

AJ felt the key in his waistcoat pocket.

Mr. Stone relit his pipe. A whirl of smoke hid his features. "The door must be locked by a Jobey, and locked forever, from this side or the other. The question is, Mr. Jobey, on which side do you belong? Here in the past or in the future?"

CHAPTER 11

"Can I think about it? I might want to come back and look around."

"I would urge you, Mr. Jobey, to return to your own time and stay there," said Mr. Stone. "Lock the door behind you when you leave, and put the key through the letter box."

"Why would I want to do that?"

Mr. Stone looked at AJ as if he were a simpleton.

"Have you ever heard of Janus, Mr. Jobey?"

"No," said AJ.

"He is an ancient Roman god with two identical faces, one that sees into the future, the other into the past. The guardian of doorways, he does not take kindly to those who cross Time's threshold. Old Jobey, your grandfather, paid no heed to my words of advice. He found he had a lucrative trade with the twentieth century. He sent his son there when he became too infirm to go himself. Too late, he decided to lock the door. He wanted Lucas back where he belonged. But the damage was done and the key lost."

AJ shivered.

"The two stone faces above the door."

"Yes, Mr. Jobey, one on each side. They are there to remind all who hold the key of their duty to the past and to the future. I advise you to do as you are told. It is for the best." He handed AJ a small box. "It has been a pleasure to meet Old Jobey's grandson. Please accept this very fine snuffbox as a token of our gratitude for bringing the key back to its rightful place."

AJ knew when he was being fobbed off. There was more going on here than some pathetic story about some old Roman geezer he had never heard of who held a grudge about being Time's bouncer. He found his hand had instinctively tightened round the key, and he made up his mind not to let it go.

"So that's it?" said AJ. "You want me to lock Jobey's Door and post the key back. Then what?"

"Nothing," said Mr. Stone. "All will be as it should be."

"But the key is rightfully mine—you said so. Goods and chattels and all that."

"Ah . . . rightfully yours until you pass it back through the door. Then, by the terms of your grandfather's will, it reverts to the custody of Groat Stone. It will be destroyed, and the future and the past will have no more inconvenient leakages. And you, Mr. Jobey, will not be tempted to repeat the fatal mistakes of your grandfather and father."

"Hold on a minute. In my life I've never had much chance to dream, and the dreams I have had have amounted to nothing. Now that I've come across the improbable impossible, you want me to come over all Boy Scout and hand the key back to you? For a snuffbox? You must be joking."

"I am sure the past has little to offer a young man of your talents."

Mr. Stone returned to his desk and his four eyes returned to the book in which he had been writing.

"I think you'd be surprised," said AJ.

Outside the sun was lazily rising as London washed the sleep from her eyes.

"Bloody hell," said AJ. "Who would believe this?"

He looked back at the long slab of buildings he had just left. Overhead, the scrawl of gulls, white against a gray sky. The bells of St. Clements rang, and clerks in hats and mufflers rushed through the gate to work, just as they did in his own time. The difference was the absence of the electronic jungle. Here life was raw, rude and real.

"What year is it? I mean, here?" asked AJ as he and Ingleby set off towards Farringdon Road.

"The year is 1830. The old king, George, died in June and William is our new king. The Duke of Wellington is prime minister."

"Where does Charles Dickens live?" asked AJ.

"Never heard of him. And if you are going to tell me something about the future I would rather you didn't. I have always been superstitious: hats on beds, shoes on tables. The future isn't for knowing."

By now the streets were beginning to fill with bustle and clatter. This was the same London AJ knew, had always known; the same and yet it was a foreign country.

"Mr. Ingleby," called someone in the crowd. "Mr. Ingleby, wait."

Coming towards them was a young woman. Though walking

quickly, she didn't wave or run but seemed confident that her voice alone would attract Ingleby's attention.

"Miss Esme," said Ingleby. "What finds you up so early?"

"Mr. Ingleby, I was on my way to your house. It is my father. He has been taken ill and is asking for you."

"Asking for me?" said Ingleby. "Why on earth does he ask for me?"

"There is something he wants to tell you. I don't know what it is. He has been feeling unwell for several days, but yesterday morning he came down with a fever so severe that he took to his bed. By the afternoon he was complaining of pains in his stomach and that he found breathing hard. Mrs. Meacock called for Dr. Seagrave to come. He did, and bled my father to no good effect, and now he is worse. The doctor doesn't think he will see the day out."

"What does the doctor think ails him?" asked Ingleby.

"He cannot be sure, but he says the symptoms are similar to those found in cholera."

"Cholera?" repeated Ingleby. "I hope for all our sakes that the doctor is wrong. So far London has been spared that disease. It seems unlikely that your father should be its first victim in the city."

"I agree," said Miss Esme. She looked Ingleby straight in the eye and said, "I believe he has been poisoned. Last night he became more agitated. I sat with him, and twice he tried to leave his bed saying that he would not rest until he had spoken to you and only you. Mrs. Meacock said he was delirious and we should ignore him. This morning he pulled me close and whispered, 'Bring Ingleby—do it now.'"

AJ could tell that Ingleby was torn. He had been given his orders, and they were to take AJ back to the house in Clerkenwell. It was obvious that he wasn't keen to visit a man who was suspected of dying of cholera. AJ wasn't keen to be late for work, but an experience like this didn't happen every day.

Miss Esme said quietly, "My father keeps saying if he doesn't see you he will take his secret to the grave and then the truth will be forever buried."

These words had an immediate effect on Ingleby's indecision, and he waved down a hackney cab.

"St. John Street, and be fast about it!" he shouted. "Mr. Jobey, I doubt we are going to the house of a cholera victim, but who knows."

"We won't catch it," said AJ. "It's spread through filthy water."

"Well, that is reassuring," said Ingleby.

"Are you a doctor?" asked Miss Esme.

"No," said AJ.

"Then how do you know so much about this terrible plague? Have you been following the news from Moscow, where so many people have died? They say it is only a matter of time until London is affected. I have read nothing about water, only that you catch it from the smell in the air."

"That's rubbish," said AJ. "Anyway, if I remember rightly, cholera won't reach here until the end of next year."

Ingleby let out a loud and meaningful cough.

"My friend here has some far-fetched ideas. Ahead of his time, you might say."

"I didn't catch your name," said Miss Esme.

"Mr. Jobey is soon to be gone from the metropolis," said Ingleby. "Abroad," he added.

AJ smiled at the young woman and she turned away and looked out the window.

He sat, taking it all in, recording every detail with his senses—his eyes, his ears, his touch. He missed nothing: the battered leather seats that smelled of horse, stables and tobacco; the way the carriage went hard over the bumps; the noise of the street criers; the snorting of horses; metal-rimmed wheels clattering over cobbles.

"Where are we?" he asked.

"Coming up to Clerkenwell Green," replied Ingleby.

"Have you never been this way before, Mr. Jobey?" said Miss Esme.

"It's much changed since I was last here," said AJ.

Strange, thought AJ. If her old dad is about to hang up his clogs forever, shouldn't she be a tad more upset? She seemed so calm. He tried to think how he would feel if the red reptile was on her deathbed. Yep. Maybe he would be sitting there just like this girl, staring out the window, loving the sun of a new day.

The carriage drew up outside a tall, grand house in St. John Street, and Miss Esme led them in. The hall was in darkness. The door of the dining room stood ajar, and an unpleasant smell wafted from it. AJ glanced in. A couple of chairs had been knocked over, and on the floor, silver and china were scattered all around. A linen tablecloth was covered in bloody vomit. It certainly looked like something not altogether honest had been going on.

A woman appeared on the stairs. In the gloom it was hard to see her face. She was small, and nothing about her said welcome. This must be Mrs. Meacock, thought AJ.

"Mr. Ingleby. You should not be here," the woman said.

"My father requested I bring him," interrupted Miss Esme, her voice tight.

"There was no need, no need at all. I told you to leave well alone, dear." The woman smiled at the girl but her eyes simmered with rage. "I am sorry, Mr. Ingleby. Miss Esme has these flights of fancy. They seem to be occurring more frequently. Unfortunately Mr. Dalton is too ill to see anyone."

Dalton, thought AJ. Mr. Stone said Old Jobey's business partner was called Samuel Dalton.

A woman came up from the basement carrying a jug of steaming water. Just then there was a cry from upstairs.

"Ingleby! Is he here?"

To AJ's surprise Mrs. Meacock barred everyone from going up and told the woman with the jug to stay in the kitchen.

"I will call you when you're needed, dear Mrs. Renwick," she said sweetly.

As far as AJ could see, the best thing they could do was call for the emergency services. He had to remind himself where he was, and he was wondering what would happen next when Ingleby said firmly, "Out of my way, madam," and ran up the stairs.

"But Mr. Dalton might well be infectious," said the saccharine-voiced housekeeper.

AJ noticed that all the while she had her hand on the girl. He followed them up to Mr. Dalton's bedchamber.

This, like the dining room, had been trashed—the hangings of the four-poster bed lay on the floor. The man in the bed pulled himself upright, his hands reaching out to Ingleby. Then he stopped and stared wide-eyed at AJ, as if he'd seen a ghost.

"Have you come for me?" he shouted, pointing at AJ. "I tell you, I knew nothing of it, that is the honest truth. I asked for none of it. None of it."

"I fear it might be cholera," Mrs. Meacock said, stroking his brow. "That is why it is not safe for any of you to be in this room. I must ask you all to leave."

"Too late, you're too late!" cried Mr. Dalton. "It's all done with."

He collapsed on the pillows.

Why was no doctor present? AJ wondered—and he noted something else about this uncomfortable scene. Miss Esme was staring out the window, as if oblivious to her father's distress.

"Where's the doctor?" AJ whispered to her. "At least a nurse should be here."

"The doctor said he would be back in an hour with more medicine, but we have yet to see him."

Again Mr. Dalton rose, and again he pointed at AJ.

"Have you come to take your revenge?"

Mrs. Meacock turned on Ingleby.

"There," she said. "You are only making matters worse. Miss Esme should never have brought you."

She pulled vigorously on a velvet rope beside the bed.

Mrs. Renwick appeared at the door with the same jug of boiling water, and the housekeeper shooed them all from the room.

"See what you have done, my dear?" she said to Miss Esme.

Ingleby didn't wait to hear more. He pulled AJ out of the house and onto the street, where he hailed another hackney cab.

"That man used to work with my grandfather, didn't he?" said AJ. "So why did he want to see you so badly?"

"Best you forget all you have seen, best by far," said Ingleby.

"No," said AJ. "Why did he think he knew me? Did he think I was my father?"

Ingleby didn't answer.

At the tumbledown house where AJ's adventure had started the night before, Ingleby said as he opened the door, "No need to go upstairs. Your clothes are in a bundle on that chair. Now, when I let you out, just close the door behind you and you will find yourself back where you came from."

"Not so fast," said AJ. "I'm going, but first answer my questions."

"Mr. Jobey," said Ingleby, "my advice to you is to lock the door, post the key through the letter box and let the past well alone."

CHAPTER 12

AJ felt grubby and decided he would have a wash and shave before he went to work. It was a choice between two evils: he turned up for work on time looking like a scruffball or he turned up for work late, washed and shaved. Either way Morton's disapproval would fall on him like a ton of bricks.

"Where've you been?" said Leon.

"Out," said AJ as he walked into the lounge of Leon's flat. Dr. Jinx was sitting surrounded by beer cans and empty pizza cartons. He looked as if he had been gradually simmering into the sofa over a long period of time. As far as AJ was concerned Jinx was the rat of the neighborhood. A rat with a Glaswegian accent so thick that you could cut off its tail with a carving knife. Both his cheeks were tattooed with skulls; his eyebrows, nose and upper lip were all pierced. Since he'd become a father seven years before, he had started to take his business a tad more seriously, and these days he dressed with attitude to show the punters he was doing all right: a red tartan suit with drainpipe trousers, a small porkpie hat on the top of his spiky green hair.

"I am unforgettable," he would say. "So unforgettable that no one can remember me."

AJ didn't like Dr. Jinx one little bit.

"What's he doing here, bro?" he asked Leon.

"Now, that's not a nice way to talk about Dr. Jinx, is it, wee man?"

"Do you deserve nice? I don't think so," said AJ. "I can't imagine that nice and you have ever met."

"Wee cocky bastard. You'd better watch that tongue of yours, laddie. Now piss off. I have business with Leon." His words drifted away in a long exhale of smoke. He stubbed out his cigarette on a half-eaten pizza. "Been to a fancy-dress party? You look out of it."

He stood up to leave and Leon followed him into the hall. AJ heard Dr. Jinx say, "Don't let me down. Six at Blues."

Blues was a billiards club that none of them had ever bothered with. It was where all trouble started.

"What are you up to?" asked AJ when Leon came back into the lounge.

"Making a living, bro," said Leon, flopping down into a chair. "Paying the rent, that kind of shit."

"I said I'd help."

"Yeah. But I want more, bro."

"Don't we all," said AJ. He moved the pizza cartons and opened the window to let out the stink of Jinx's cheap aftershave.

"You know that's your mum's dealer—the one who sold her the smack in the first place. What are you doing?"

"Shut it. You sound like a nagging girl. I do my stuff, you

do yours. Live and let live, OK?" said Leon. "Anyway, why are you dressed like that? You escaped from some TV drama?"

AJ had been so surprised to find himself on the other side of the door that he hadn't given a thought to what he was wearing. He'd made his way out of the car park back to Mount Pleasant, clutching his secondhand suit and brogues, where he'd caught a bus back to Stokey. He'd sat on the top, huddled in the corner at the front, and, staring blankly out of the window, thought about the young girl and the dying man.

AJ felt for the key, checked that he still had the snuffbox, and decided that, come the weekend, he'd go back and check things out by himself.

"So where have you been?" asked Leon. "And where did you find those clothes?"

"You wouldn't believe me if I told you. Tea?" said AJ, going into the kitchen and putting on the kettle.

Leon followed him.

"Have you seem Slim?" he asked.

"No. Why?"

"He came round last night. Said he was in *lo-ove* and his girl *lo-oved* him so much that she wanted him to give up skateboarding."

AJ found two cups without mold growing in the bottom and put the tea bags in them.

"Has to be black," he said. "The milk's off."

"Whatever," said Leon.

"Who is she?" asked AJ.

"Sicknote."

"What?" said AJ. "You are joking, man. Sicknote? No, she'll use him and abuse him."

"I know that, you know that. The only person who doesn't know it is Slim. She's Moses's girl. Slim doesn't want to go crossing Moses. Moses will eat him for breakfast and Sicknote won't give a monkey's. Didn't he text you?"

AJ took his mobile out of his pocket and saw he had one missed call and two texts. He also saw the time—it was nearly nine-thirty.

"Damn. I should have been at work an hour ago."

One text was from Slim, the other from work; the call was from his mum.

He read the text from Morton.

"You are not needed in chambers until ten o'clock."

There was still time. He might just make it without being too late. He rushed into the bathroom to shave and brush his teeth. In his bedroom he pulled his office suit over the cambric shirt and waistcoat and put the key in the pocket of his jacket.

"Forget Dr. Jinx," he said, poking his head round the lounge door. "He's nothing but trouble. Here, see if you can do something with this."

He threw Leon the snuffbox.

"Sweet," said Leon, examining it. "Where did you get it?"

"Later," shouted AJ as he closed the front door behind him.

The voice mail from his mum was typical. He couldn't just walk out on her like that. She needed his rent whether he was there or not. The message ended with "Frank says so."

The text from Slim was a mess. He had changed his Facebook page to say that he and Sicknote were an item.

If his two best friends had been looking for trouble, they had been unbelievably successful in finding it.

It was ten past ten when he arrived at Raymond Buildings. A half-exposed photograph of another century overlaid Gray's Inn.

"Late!" shouted Morton from the clerk's office.

"Sorry," said AJ. "The bus . . ."

"Don't let it happen again."

"It won't."

"Good. Detective Poilaine wants to see you."

"Why?" said AJ, feeling as if he was wading into a sea of panic and would probably drown there.

"The hospital tests confirmed that Mr. Baldwin was poisoned. Everyone in chambers has been interviewed except you. Just answer the questions; then you'll be going back to the Old Bailey. Ms. Finch wants you, she— What are you wearing, Mr. Jobey? It is an eccentric look, and one not altogether suitable for a baby clerk in these chambers. And where is your tie?"

Detective Poilaine wore a sharp gray suit and high heels and had a turned-up nose. She didn't look as if she belonged in the police at all. The interview took place in the Museum, and AJ feared that at any moment the files would start talking of their own accord and he would be busted. He just hoped that he wouldn't have to tell too many lies. Fortunately, he was able to say truthfully that he'd last seen Mr. Baldwin on Friday morning. It was the longest ten minutes of his life.

"Interesting waistcoat, Mr. Jobey," said the detective as he left the room.

Morton handed him a file.

"There's a taxi downstairs waiting to take you to the Old Bailey. Give this to Ms. Finch immediately."

AJ was out of Raymond Buildings as fast as a dog from a trap. In the back of the cab, trying to catch his breath, he wondered if he should have told the truth. What truth? He would have thought he'd dreamed the whole thing if it wasn't for the waistcoat and shirt he was wearing. When he thought about it, daydreaming had been a big problem at school. It did him no favors, so his teacher had told him.

"You can't let dreams rule your life," she'd said.

He'd answered back, which was never wise.

"Reality sucks."

He'd spent the rest of the class standing in the corridor.

His mobile rang. It was Slim.

"Hi, bro," said Slim. "Where are you?"

"Working. Where are you?"

"In Topshop, waiting for my girl. I'm buying her a party dress."

"Slim, man, what are you doing? Sicknote is nothing but trouble, and Moses will kill you if he finds out you are with his girl."

"She broke up with him. This is serious."

"Yeah, seriously unwise."

It was then that AJ saw that a photo had fallen from the file.

"Have to go," said AJ, reaching down to pick it up. "Look, I'll call you later, all right?"

AJ blinked. He was tired, he was imagining things, it was all too much. His two best friends were losing the plot and he had lied to the police. Life felt like a road accident. He looked again at the photo. Apart from the clothes, the only difference between the man in the photo and the dying man he had seen that morning was that the man in the photo looked well. He turned it over. On the back was written *Samuel Dalton, April 2008*.

CHAPTER 13

It struck AJ as he got out of the cab that he was in a very sticky place. Six weeks ago he was just another sixteen-year-old who had failed his exams and was about to join the long list of the unemployable. By a fluke he'd been given a job and with it had come a pileup of unanswered questions. And a house with a front door.

"Aiden," said Ms. Finch. "The file?"

He had been so wrapped in his thoughts that he hadn't noticed her standing by the entrance to the Old Bailey.

"Yes," he said, handing it over. "Here."

"Thank you," she said. "Not that it's needed now. Mr. Purcell was taken ill last night. The case has been adjourned for two weeks. Coffee?"

A croissant and a hot chocolate with whipped cream helped to fill the gargantuan hole in AJ's stomach.

"How did Mr. Purcell know the man in the photograph, Samuel Dalton?" asked AJ, licking the cream off his spoon.

"He claims that Samuel Dalton and he were business partners, but unfortunately for our client, we have been unable to trace any record of the existence of this Samuel Dalton. Mr. Purcell insists that he knew Mr. Dalton, hence the photo, which was taken outside his flat. He also insists that he saw documentation showing the snuffboxes were genuine. Unfortunately, according to Mr. Purcell, those documents are with Samuel Dalton. We go round and round in circles." Ms. Finch sighed. "Mr. Baldwin said he wasn't worried about the documentation. He said that he would have it by the end of this week. Now he is in hospital and we have a missing witness and a hell of a lot of unexplained original eighteenth-century snuffboxes. So where does it all lead us?"

"I would say," said AJ, "up shit creek."

It was five o'clock when Morton asked to see AJ in his office. Once again AJ's stomach started its unhelpful roller-coaster ride. He was sure that Detective Poilaine had spotted a lie and Morton was going to say he should tell the truth if he wanted to keep his job. He even thought that the key in his pocket might be obvious and Morton had sussed out that he had it. Thinking through all the possible ramifications, he was completely unprepared for what Morton did have to say.

"Do you get on well with Mr. Baldwin?"

AJ was puzzled.

"I make him his coffee, that's all."

Morton wrote something on his notepad, tore out the page and handed it to AJ.

"Room twenty-seven, the London Clinic."

"What's this?" asked AJ.

"It's where Mr. Baldwin is being treated, and, strange as it may seem—and believe me, it seems strange to me—he has asked to see you. So you are to take a taxi and go there now. That's all."

"Do I take flowers?"

"No," said Morton.

"Mr. Jobey," said a nurse. "You may go in."

Mr. Baldwin was in intensive care in a smallish room that you weren't allowed in until you had washed your hands and were wearing a plastic apron. This and the morning visit to Samuel Dalton couldn't have been at further ends of two worlds. To AJ, both felt as unreal as the other. The cold light and the endless blip-bleep of the monitors had more life in them than the patient. The place was as hot as a lizard's aquarium. Mr. Baldwin was tubed and wired, his mouth covered in a plastic mask. Two nurses were reading charts and checking the monitors. For all that, his condition looked not unlike Mr. Dalton's.

AJ had never visited anyone in hospital before and had no idea what he was supposed to do. He stood awkwardly at the end of the bed.

"Hello, Mr. Baldwin. You sent for me."

The QC's eyes were closed, and he didn't appear to be up for any profound conversation.

"Why don't you sit down," said a nurse kindly.

AJ did, and a tidal wave of tiredness overtook him. He hadn't slept in so long, and the atmosphere in the room wasn't exactly conducive to being alert. He must have nodded off, but he woke with a start as soon as he heard his name. The mask that had been on Mr. Baldwin's face had been taken off.

"You have five minutes and no longer, Mr. Baldwin," said the nurse, looking anxiously at her patient.

Mr. Baldwin waved her away.

"Listen to me, and listen carefully," he said to AJ, his tight words held together by a lack of emotion. "This is important. The documentation that authenticates the snuffboxes in the Purcell case is at Samuel Dalton's house in Clerkenwell. Do you know where that is?"

Lying seemed pointless. AJ nodded.

"I take it Ingleby found you?"

AJ nodded again.

Baldwin's tongue flicked in and out of his mouth.

"It is imperative that you find the papers and give them to Ms. Finch. They are vital to the defense of our client. Do you understand?"

"Yes, sir," said AJ.

"Good. I am fighting this sickness, and I will win. I am not going to die, Aiden—neither am I going to lose the case or my reputation." A hand with a drip attached to it grabbed hold of AJ's arm with unexpected strength. "Have you locked the door?"

"No, sir."

"So you have the key, then. Whatever you do, do not lock the door. When you've found the papers you will return the key to me. And you will mention it to no one, no one. It will be our secret, and I will take the matter of your stealing it no further. Your job—your future—will be secure. Do I make myself clear?"

AJ nodded.

Baldwin closed his eyes.

The nurse came back and fitted the mask over the lawyer's mouth. The visit was over.

Outside, the toxic fumes of Marylebone Road smelled good, and AJ took deep gulps. Everything had gone badly. Perhaps the professor would be able to put him straight about a few things. He should be at the café at Rosebery Avenue by now.

AJ fell asleep on the bus. His phone woke him up, and he was relieved to see Slim's familiar number. The sky exploded with rockets trailing stars of light. AJ had forgotten it was Guy Fawkes Night.

"Where are you?" Slim said.

"On my way back from work. What's up? Is everything all right?"

There was silence at the other end. Another firework roared into the sky.

"Slim," said AJ. "Is it Moses?"

"No, nothing like that. Look, my phone is about to crash. I've something to . . ."

Slim's phone died. AJ tried to call him back but couldn't get through. By the time he had arrived at Mount Pleasant he had put Slim's call out of his mind.

AJ found the café the professor had taken him to. He had the change from the taxi fare, and he went in, sat down at a table by the window and used it to fund a feast.

"May I join you?"

"Bloody hell! Where did you spring from?" said AJ.

"A nice waistcoat and a shirt of the finest cambric," said the professor, sitting down. "Have your wages gone up, AJ?"

"No."

"Then you now know the answer to the riddle of my pocket watch."

AJ drank his tea.

"I now have several riddles, all of which have one thing in common: a key. It seems that I have the only key to a door, and I am the only person who can lock it, but at this moment it's open to anyone who knows about it. Mr. Baldwin said that unless I return the key to him he is going to bust me, and Mr. Stone with four eyes said I must lock the door and post the key back."

The professor interrupted him.

"But you haven't, have you, AJ?"

"Haven't what?"

"Haven't locked the door and posted the key through the letter box?"

The professor's eyes never left AJ's.

"No. I still have it on me."

The professor sighed.

"I am glad to hear that. Another pot of tea, please," he called to the man behind the counter.

"Coming up, professor."

"Now, tell me slowly and precisely what has happened and where you have been."

AJ told him about meeting Ingleby and Stone, and being taken to Samuel Dalton's house, and about his recent interview with Mr. Baldwin.

"I tell you, some weird shit is going on. Now I don't know who to trust or even how many people know about the door.

This is far more complicated than anything Beanstalk Jack ever had to deal with."

At that moment AJ's phone rang. It was Slim.

"Hi, bro. Phone ran out of juice."

"Later," said AJ.

"No," said Slim. "This is important. You need to come back."

"Why? I'm busy."

There was a pause, and for a moment AJ thought Slim's phone was dropping out again. He could hardly hear him for the whizz-bangs. One lone spectacular wheel illuminated the sky with falling diamonds.

"Because," said Slim, "Leon's mum is dead."

CHAPTER 14

AJ had never been on a plane, never been to a foreign land; only London muck had ever stuck to the soles of his shoes. He had no idea what jet lag felt like, but he wondered if he could be suffering from time lag.

Whatever it was, everything was unreal. Leon, Leon's mum, Slim—all seemed to float about him. He felt sick with tiredness, so much so that he had fallen asleep again on the bus and missed his stop at Stoke Newington Town Hall and had to catch another bus back from Stamford Hill.

Slim was waiting outside the Rose and Crown, uncomfortably puffing on a cigarette.

"You don't smoke," said AJ.

"Leon's gone missing," said Slim, stubbing out the cigarette. He stopped and looked at AJ. "You all right? You're gray."

"Had a hard day," said AJ, wishing he had been with Leon instead of chasing a mystery he didn't have a hope of ever understanding. "What do you mean, gone missing?"

Slim sighed. "It's messed up. Auntie Elsie went to the hospital with him, and that was when they turned off his mum's life support. The social services were there too. Leon told them he needed a piss and that was the last anyone saw of him. Now the police are round at his flat."

"Shit," said AJ.

"Yeah, life is shitty, it sure ain't pretty. The vultures have descended. Margot from Ranger Housing Association is up there too. The rent was months overdue. Seems like Leon has lost his mum and his home, all with the click of a switch. His mum was more use as a living vegetable than a corpse."

"Ever thought of being a poet?" said AJ. "Come on, we'd better try to find Leon."

"I've been looking all day. Down at Blues, on the South Bank—nothing. And I can't search anymore, man," Slim said sheepishly. "Sorry, bro, I'm taking my girl out."

"What are you on?" said AJ. "Leon's mum has died and you are determined to add to the sum total of misery by going out with the girlfriend of the nastiest piece of manhood that was ever assembled in the factory of life. Moses is a basket case."

"She's finished with him for good."

"I doubt that, bro. I imagine Sicknote is making sure she has one of her Gucci stilettos in each camp. Why do you want to be involved with the bitch?"

"Don't call her that. I love her. Don't laugh."

"I'm not laughing."

"You see, I've had this crush on her since—"

"Since you lost the will to live?" said AJ. "Oh, give me strength. There's no Cupid's bow waiting for you, mate, just Moses's flick knife and you know it. It's pathetic."

"Shut it," said Slim. "Just shut it." He took out another cigarette and lit it with an unsteady hand. "Got to go."

Walking towards them, in a gaggle of glittering girls, was Sicknote, the Cleopatra of Stokey, coming to claim her slave.

Slim threw the cigarette away.

AJ looked on, disgusted, as Slim almost ran to her.

"Just be careful, that's all," he said to no one in particular.

Outside Leon's block, AJ found Leon's sofa leaning against the wall along with two mattresses and several black bin bags. His clothes were mixed up with the rubbish. They all stank. So that was that. For what it was worth, Rangers had reclaimed the dump. There was no point in seeing if he could get in. Anyway, it was dark and hard to see with eyes that needed matchsticks to keep them open. He focused on his oversized brogues. One step, two steps, three. He had to put his faith in something, and shoes seemed a good bet. He saw Moses's gang hanging out in the doorway.

Keep your eyes off those geezers and concentrate on the shoes, he thought. They were moving in the general direction of Bodman House. He rang Elsie's bell.

Dear old Elsie. London may tumble, St. Paul's might crumble, but Elsie would always be there. She'd been just a little kid during the Blitz, had seen the houses round about go down. She even had an uncle Stan who had been shot by a Stuka on Church Street.

"He was a stubborn bugger," she'd said. "He wouldn't lie down on the pavement when the plane flew overhead—he just stood in the road with his fingers in a V-sign and, lo and behold, if that Stuka didn't double back and shoot him full of holes. No one else, just my uncle Stan. Daft as a brush, he was."

Elsie opened the door.

"Give me those," she said, taking his smelly clothes. "Cup of tea? You're all done in. What a day, what a day. I take it you haven't seen Leon?"

"No. I'll have the tea and then I'm going out searching and I will find him."

The idea that you could just boil water and make tea at the flick of a switch struck him for the first time in his life as a luxury. Maybe you needed to see the past to appreciate the present.

Elsie, the queen of the practical, put both hands on her hips. She had just had her hair dyed blue, and the tightness of her curls and the lines on her face made her, in the dim light of her lounge, look beautiful to AJ.

"You . . . ," she said slowly, as if measuring out each word to see if they had the right amount of weight to them, "you are not responsible for Leon or for Slim."

AJ stood up to protest.

"I haven't finished. You need to take care of—" Elsie stopped mid-sentence. "What are you wearing?"

AJ was too muddled to understand what she was saying. Her words drifted in and out of his consciousness. She showed him into the bedroom that had once belonged to her son, Norris.

"You can stay here for a while, if you like," she said.

He took off his waistcoat and shirt and lay down on the bed, and before Elsie had brought him tea and Marmite toast, AJ was fast asleep.

The next morning he had a bath and realized that he felt

to walk its streets and be a part of it. He wanted to call on Miss Esme and ask a few important questions. Hopefully she would know where to find the documents Mr. Baldwin wanted. And he had this half-baked notion that if he could only speak to her alone, the mystery of how her father knew his father would be solved. He tossed the coin.

Tails.

"Going anywhere nice?" Elsie asked him.

"Just to look for Leon."

"All dolled up like that? I may look like I'm not all there, but I can tell a lie from fifty feet, and that one is so whopping it almost fills the lounge."

AJ sighed. "There something I have to do. It's all right, it's safe."

"As long as it's not trailing trouble behind it."

Fearing more questions, AJ left the flat with a piece of toast in his mouth and the rest of the clothes Ingleby had given him in a Sainsbury's bag.

"Don't worry," he said.

"I've heard that before," said Elsie.

AJ imagined it would be a lot harder to get into the car park at Phoenix Place in daylight than it had been at night. What he had discovered working at Baldwin Groat, though, was that a suit, however cheap, put you in a different category. You didn't look like someone who was about to spray his name on a brick wall.

He followed a worker from the sorting office through the

a human being again. A human being with a plan. He would look for Leon after work. He would find him even if it meant tackling Dr. Jinx. Elsie was in the living room, sitting in her armchair. The ironing board was out, and all AJ's clothes had been washed and pressed.

"You shouldn't have bothered," said AJ. Elsie was staring into space. "Elsie?" he said. "Are you all right?"

"Where did you find those?" she said, pointing to the shirt and waistcoat Ingleby had given him.

"Oh—I don't know."

"That's what Norris said when I asked him the same question, a week before he went missing."

"Norris, your son?"

"Yes," said Elsie. She stood up and went into the kitchen. "Coffee?"

Some things are so important that getting the right information demands asking the right question. AJ had to give the question some thought. He waited until Elsie had put coffee and cereal on the kitchen table.

"You mean your son, Norris, had these very same clothes?" said AJ.

"That's about the sum of it," said Elsie. "I told the police about them, but they weren't interested." She took a sip of her coffee. "Lucas was supposed to come back to live with your mum. He said he just had to sort something out. When he never came back, Norris said he would go looking for him. That was the last time I saw my son. And no one ever saw Lucas Jobey again either."

It had never occurred to AJ that Elsie might have known his father.

"You knew my father?" He said the words quietly, as if the sound of them might frighten away the answer.

"I did," said Elsie. "But it was a long time ago."

CHAPTER 15

AJ opened his eyes on Saturday morning and though mess. He had looked for Leon every evening after no success, and today he planned to devote his who finding him. Even as he thought it he knew he would to. Somehow he had to retrieve the papers Mr. Baldw He dreaded what would happen if miraculously M was out of hospital on Monday. The first thing the la do would be to demand the key and the documen the second thing he would do would be to fire hi

"Shit, shit."

AJ was wide-awake—no long lie-in this morning out of bed. He washed and put his suit on over waistcoat. There was a clank as a penny rolle waistcoat pocket. It was large and old, with a pictu IV on one side and *Rule Britannia* on the other. I on it: 1825. This was a good sign. It was the sai the stone above the doors to 4 Raymond Build

Heads I look for my best mate and blow the he thought; tails I go back through Jobey's D longing to be there again, to feel that other Lon

side gate into the car park. A little way off a car alarm began a constant whine.

Gradually he became aware that the needy wail had faded away. A fog enfolded him and the red door appeared, as did the stone face and the hand of the knocker. He almost ran at it, imagining its hinges to be stiff as before, only to find that the door opened with such ease that he almost lost his footing. Once he was in the hall the door closed behind him and he could hear the meow of a cat, the clip-clop of horses' hooves outside but nothing else, only the silence that belonged to a house in another century.

The hall had a fraction more light in it than it had at night. The place felt coffin-still.

"Hello?" he called.

He was half hoping that Ingleby would be there. He wouldn't have minded a chat with him. He changed his clothes, left his suit and mobile in the cupboard under the stairs and picked up his hat and muffler. He opened the door again. Fingers crossed he wasn't going out into the Phoenix Place car park.

"Bloody hell," he said to himself.

He had arrived in the nineteenth century.

A frost had settled over this London, and the air was bitter and clear. The city was so transformed in the daylight that it took his breath away. The gray dome of St. Paul's loomed through the rolling drifts of murky smoke from a thousand chimney pots.

In his world St. Paul's could just be seen from his mum's balcony, dwarfed by the Shard and the Gherkin—the great-great-great-grandfather of London surrounded by its precocious children. Here, Christopher Wren's building stood tall above rooftops, a landmark by which he could take his bearings.

He walked towards Clerkenwell through a London that no longer existed, dawdling, taking it all in. It smelled raw: poverty and grandeur nestled together. The shopfronts were small, some decorated, some undecorated, with nothing to show what they were selling. The noise of the city was deafening. A brewer's dray came along, making more din than AJ thought possible; a sedan chair wobbled past, the passenger a lady with a painted face and a tall white wig, protesting that the porters were too slow. This was the London he'd read about, and somewhere here lived his hero, Charles Dickens. He wouldn't have yet written *Sketches by Boz*, let alone *Pickwick Papers*. Dickens must be about eighteen and, if AJ remembered correctly, was working as a reporter.

"Wow," said AJ to himself. "What a day."

He laughed when he saw the stagecoaches, beautifully turned out, driving merrily through the streets. There were no traffic lights to stop them. There were no police to keep order. London had a chaos of its own making, and it seemed to work. He passed street merchants crying out their wares, things AJ would buy at the local corner shop. Finally he reached St. John Street.

He wasn't sure which house it was that Ingleby had taken him to. He thought he had walked past it until a door opened and AJ recognized the housekeeper, Mrs. Meacock. She stood for a moment on the front step but didn't notice him. Or so he hoped. Picasso could have had this woman in mind when he made his Cubist portraits, for her face had many sides to it and not one would AJ trust. She glanced up at the first-floor window and so did AJ. There stood Miss Esme Dalton.

He waited in a doorway, and only when Mrs. Meacock had vanished in the direction of Smithfield Market did he emerge to find that Miss Esme was no longer at the window.

His plan took courage. He would knock on the front door and ask to speak to her. But his courage turned from a bulldog into a Chihuahua.

Bad idea. Did he think he could just say, "Hi, I was wondering if you know anything about these papers your father had? They're to do with some priceless snuffboxes."

Even as he said it to himself he realized the whole thing sounded nuts.

"Gingerbread, hot gingerbread!" shouted a young lad wearing a hat far too big for him.

AJ was about to walk away, but, stuffing his hands in his pockets, he found some coins there.

"Yes," he said to the boy. "One, please, mate."

"Perhaps you would make that two, Mr. Jobey?" said a voice behind him.

AJ turned. Miss Esme stood in the doorway, wrapped in a shawl.

"Two," said AJ. "And keep the change."

He wasn't sure if he had underpaid or overpaid.

"I think you have just bought all his gingerbread and the basket," said Miss Esme, solemnly.

AJ hadn't properly seen her before. She was tall, willowy, with a face that looked out of place, belonging more to the twenty-first century than the nineteenth. They walked in an uncomfortable silence and ate the gingerbread.

Why had he ever imagined this would be easy? Nothing—past, present or future—is ever easy.

"Mr. Jobey, may I enquire . . . ," she said slowly, then stopped and glanced behind her. "Mr. Jobey, why have you come here?"

"To buy you gingerbread."

She smiled, and it was a smile that changed her face into something altogether softer, less corseted. Her eyes were a gentle gray in her pale face; her hair hung straight in two heavy curtains that had resisted all attempts to curl them. He had noticed that the fashion seemed to be for ringlets and bonnets.

"I thought you were about to go abroad."

"A last-minute change of plan." And then he said what he shouldn't have said—it sounded so corny, like something Slim might have said: "Can't resist a pretty face."

That made her smile.

The further they walked away from St. John Street, the more she began to talk. Then, quite suddenly, she stopped and, staring at him said, "Do you ever think you were born into the wrong time?"

"Often," he said, smiling.

"Truthfully? You are not mocking me, Mr. Jobey?"

"No. I think about it a lot. Which time do you think you belong in?"

"The future," she said, without hesitation. "I think then

women might have lives of their own. Have you read the works of William Blake?"

"Yes. 'Tyger! Tyger! Burning bright . . .' "

"Very good, Mr. Jobey, but I was thinking more of his philosophy."

For a moment he thought she was going to shut up shop and stop talking altogether. Why had he been so stupid? Any fool can quote "The Tyger."

"Blake talked about doors of perception," said AJ.

"Yes," she said, once more alight with passion. "'If the doors of perception were cleansed, everything would appear to man as it is, infinite.' "

How right he was, thought AJ. Perhaps Blake'd had a door that led to the future. That didn't seem as far-fetched as it would have done a week ago.

"He writes about freedom," said Miss Esme. "A freedom to be oneself. I tell myself stories about how my life might be. Do you think me mad to believe that in the future there might be hope for women?"

"No, not at all. I'd just forgotten that Blake . . ." He was going to say "was already published" but stopped himself in time. "I'd forgotten that Blake was so wise."

They were nearing Clerkenwell Green. AJ changed the subject.

"I must apologize—I should have asked how your father is," he said.

"He died a few hours after you were last here," said Miss Esme.

"I'm sorry to hear that," said AJ. "This is a bit awkward. You see, your father recognized me, but I'd never seen him before in my life. Do you know who he thought I was?"

"He must have mistaken you for someone he used to know."

"But why should that have made him sit bolt upright like that? He was terrified."

"I don't know," she said. "There is much that I didn't know about my father. What I do know is that I didn't like him and the feeling was mutual."

"Do you mind me asking why?" said AJ.

She said nothing, so he started again.

"Did your father know a Mr. Baldwin?"

"Oh, yes, the lawyer. He dined with my father shortly before he was taken ill. My father was anxious to amend his will."

AJ wondered if he'd had a premonition that he was about to join the daffodils.

When they parted, AJ was none the wiser as to why Samuel Dalton had been so terrified to see a man he seemed to think was Lucas Jobey. Or how he came to have his photograph taken in the twenty-first century.

In a way AJ no longer cared about the snuffbox documentation. If he was fired, so be it. He would live here, in 1830, near to Esme Dalton. He had spent the best afternoon he had ever spent with a girl. He was thrilled by how she thought.

"If the world is still turning in two hundred years, I hope it will be a kinder place," she had said to him.

Oh, Miss Esme Dalton, you could rock my world, he'd thought.

By the time he'd reached the house in Mount Pleasant,

AJ had decided that if Mr. Baldwin was back in chambers on Monday he would tell him he needed more time to find the papers.

The one thing he knew he didn't want to do was to give his key to anyone.

CHAPTER 16

The funeral of Leon's mum took place the following Wednesday. No horse-driven hearse for her—just a basic coffin, one wreath and three mourners: AJ, Slim and Elsie. No one had seen Leon since his mother had died. It wasn't for the lack of looking.

AJ had spent all of Sunday searching for him, and all he had found were rumors and gossip about Leon being in deep shit.

AJ hadn't found Leon and he hadn't found the snuffbox papers, but on Monday he had learned, to his relief, that although Mr. Baldwin's condition was stable he was expected to be in the London Clinic for a little while longer.

AJ had hoped that Leon would be at the crematorium, but he wasn't. It was off a busy main road, and the minicab driver had had to stop and ask for directions at a petrol station. The chapel itself sat adrift among a rocky sea of monuments sanitized with plastic flowers. The crem was nothing more than a clinical conveyor belt where mortal remains were turned into something more manageable.

Slim had said he would meet AJ and Elsie there.

"Why he wouldn't come in the minicab with us is beyond me," said Elsie. "It's a right trek out to this dump."

AJ had a feeling he knew the answer. It was all over Sicknote's Facebook page: pictures of her with Moses, all loved up. "My man, the one and only," she had written. Elsie was paying the cab driver when Slim emerged from behind a memorial stone, looking like death.

"Have you eaten?" said Elsie. She took a sandwich from her handbag and offered it to Slim.

"No. Yeah. I'm all right," he said.

"Eat," said Elsie.

Slim stuffed it in his mouth as the hearse bearing Leon's mum's coffin slowly pulled up.

It was a woebegone sight. Wednesdays, thought AJ, are made for woebegone sights.

"I'm glad I've saved with the Co-op," said Elsie. "When I go, I'm going in style. It'll all be catered for, down to the last egg sandwich."

The priest wanted to be done with this cremation. He looked awkward. In his hand was a laminated order of service. AJ reckoned he had picked out the one most appropriate for a drug addict.

"She was a wonderful mum," the priest said in a voice of hopelessness, "and will be much missed in her community."

So much so that she was already forgotten, thought AJ. Her flat had been cleaned out and slapped with paint and was waiting for a new family to move in.

The priest seemed relieved when at last he could press the

button, and the curtain opened as Bob Dylan croaked Leon's mum's one request. Broken head, thought AJ. Nothing but a broken life.

It was then that AJ saw the sparrow. It must have flown into the chapel by mistake and it settled on the coffin. He wished Leon was there to see it; he would have known it was a sign, a good sign. Just before the conveyor belt started with a judder and the coffin chugged into oblivion, the sparrow flew up and sat on the rafters cleaning its wings.

"That's that," said Elsie as they stood outside in the rain. There was another funeral party waiting to go in. A family affair with weeping relatives, a huge glass hearse, pallbearers and even a small lad with a bugle to play "The Last Post." So many wreaths. The largest spelled out DAD in chrysanthemums.

Elsie had told the minicab to wait. Slim said he would rather go home by tube but Elsie was insistent.

"There is no tube to Stokey," she said. "What you going to do, love? Walk back in the rain?"

"No," said Slim. His phone bleeped.

They sat, the three of them, in the back of the car.

"What're you going to do about her ashes?" asked Slim.

"I'm picking them up tomorrow," said Elsie. "I'll keep the urn in the lounge until Leon comes back. I mean, what else can we do? At least she can watch TV with me."

Slim's phone bleeped again.

AJ only now realized that Slim's phone had been bleeping all the way through the service.

Slim looked at it nervously, as if the phone itself might attack him. At Stokey Town Hall he asked the minicab to stop. He said he had something to do.

"I'd better go with him," said AJ.

"You be careful, love," said Elsie.

On the pavement Slim was as jumpy as a bag of nuclear beans.

"What's up, bro?" said AJ.

Slim handed him his phone. The last message read "if i CU your dead."

AJ scrolled down. All the messages were to do with the killing of Slim. He handed back the phone.

"Moses," he said.

Slim nodded. "Not just Moses—his whole gang are after me. And his dog. Bloody vicious, that dog, a prizefighter. It'd kill a man for a bone."

They walked together up Albion Road. After a bit AJ realized that Slim was crying.

"He's going to kill me and Sicknote doesn't care. She went back to him. She told me I was pathetic, that I didn't know nothing about ladies, that I should go back to school and learn the facts of life. Bitch. She put these pictures up on Facebook, of her and Moses. I might as well kill myself and save Moses the trouble."

"Don't say that," said AJ.

"You tried to warn me. So did Leon. I wish I was dead, man."

"What? And be stuffed in an urn?"

"What do I do? Where can I hide? This is no joke."

It came to AJ in a flash. He still had to find the documentation—there was more than a chance that Mr. Baldwin would be back in chambers any day now. Why not take Slim through the door? At least in 1830 there was no chance of Moses getting his hands on him. Yes. It might well work.

"Can you lay low until Friday?" AJ asked.

"I hope so."

"OK. On Friday I'll meet you at Phoenix Place, about six o'clock. Just be there. Oh, and make sure you've had all your jabs—measles, polio, typhoid, anything like that. Go to your GP and say you're going traveling."

"What?" said Slim. "He'll think I'm going to a jihadi training camp. Anyway, I don't have a passport."

"You won't need one," said AJ. "Not where I'm taking you."

CHAPTER 17

Once you've made it over the bump of Wednesday it's downhill all the way to Friday. And Friday couldn't come soon enough for Slim. He had phoned AJ to say that he was holed up with a cousin in Dalston. He sounded terrified and said he was too scared to go to his doctor.

"They're still after me. I tell you, man, I'm dead meat."

AJ had insisted. "Go in disguise," he said. "But go."

By Thursday Leon still hadn't been in touch. AJ felt weighed down by his friends, work, worry. Ever since he had visited Mr. Baldwin he had been as edgy as a dog with fleas. At any moment it might be reported to Morton that there was a thief working in chambers and that the thief was Aiden Jobey. He had looked up the definition of stealing online. "To take (another person's property) without permission or legal right and without intending to return it." The key had his name on it, so legally it was his property, not Baldwin's or anyone else's. It struck him—and why hadn't he thought of this before?—supposing there were hundreds of people who knew about the door and all of them were walking back and forth through time, just like it was an outing to a theme park, and helping themselves to candy? No wonder Baldwin wanted the key. No one would want to lose their free pass.

The image of a beanstalk came to him and he laughed. Jack selling tickets for all those who wished to climb up past the clouds. Somewhere through that door, he thought, a giant is waiting to eat me up. Fee-fi-fo-fum. What he didn't know was what the giant looked like.

The tension at Baldwin Groat was so thick that morning it could have been classified as toxic waste. Morton's mobile was superglued to his ear, and he was constantly in and out of meetings. Mr. Groat, who seldom put in an appearance at chambers, was now there most days except when he was in court on his partner's cases. The atmosphere was made worse by the presence of the police, who were searching Baldwin's room again.

Stephen had recovered in time to be back in the center of the maelstrom, wearing a new suit. He had lost weight, and his neck, which was long and permanently spotty, stuck out of his shirt collar. Hunched over his computer, picking at any scraps of gossip and titbits of scandal, he reminded AJ of a cartoon vulture.

"They say Mr. Baldwin's house is like a museum, full of valuable paintings and clocks from the eighteenth century."

Stephen said this to the fees clerk, who looked none too happy. Mr. Baldwin was still in intensive care, though it was reported he'd had a better night and there were slight signs of improvement. But the suspicion that someone had attempted to murder him was proving bad for business.

"Mr. Basil called Mr. Groat this morning," added Stephen. "He's taking his client's case elsewhere. Not the first, and I doubt it will be the last. There'll be departures here soon."

Morton stuck his head round the clerks' room door.

"Stephen," he said, "if anyone is going to depart, you will be the first in line. Aiden, my office, please."

AJ noted that Morton's office, never exactly tidy, was in complete turmoil.

"Is everything going to be all right?" asked AJ.

Morton sighed. "I suppose it depends which end of the bottle you're looking through. It'll be all right for someone, but not necessarily us."

AJ didn't know what he meant. It took him a moment to realize that what Morton was saying had nothing to do with Mr. Baldwin.

"Mr. Groat is summing up a libel case at the High Court. Take him these papers. You are to stay with him unless he sends you back. Oh, and, Aiden, I found this in Mr. Baldwin's office." He handed AJ a file. "Lord knows what he was doing with it. Would you put it back in the Museum?"

It was the file marked *Jobey 1813*. AJ looked inside. The map was gone.

AJ turned to leave and Morton followed him into reception, where Detective Poilaine was waiting to see him. AJ thought it best to avoid eye contact with her, although he could feel her staring at him.

"I understand you want to look at the diary," said Morton. "We have chambers to run, you know. Aiden, what are you waiting for? Cinderella's coach?"

AJ arrived at the High Court to find Mr. Groat pacing up and down the corridor outside, his hands behind his back.

"Ah, Aiden. At last."

In his wig and gown he looked even more like the man in the portrait that hung above his desk.

AJ, forgetting his place, said, "That painting above your desk, sir—is it of a relative?"

Mr. Groat glanced up.

"Yes," he said. "He was a judge at the Old Bailey—sent more men to the gallows than you've had hot dinners."

"How did he live with himself?"

"Different times, Aiden. A man—or a woman—could swing for a loaf of bread."

Mr. Groat and his team were acting for a film star who was suing a newspaper. It was an interesting case, and AJ watched from the side of the court. It took his mind off the impossibility of the instructions Mr. Baldwin had given him. Twice he was sent back to chambers to bring other documents. When court was adjourned for the day, AJ collected the files, packed away the wigs and gowns and made sure Mr. Groat had all the correct papers in his briefcase.

He was expecting to push the cart back to chambers alone, but Mr. Groat accompanied him up Chancery Lane.

"What are you reading at the moment?" he asked.

"*Our Mutual Friend*, sir," said AJ.

"Wonderful. One of my very favorites—Dickens's description of the Thames, the finding of the body . . ."

AJ had been wondering if he would ever have the chance to

ask Mr. Groat if he had known his father. In the street light of Gray's Inn, late on that Thursday afternoon, he took the plunge.

"Mr. Groat," he said, "did you ever meet my father?"

"Lucas Jobey? Yes, I did. Although he was Baldwin's client, not mine. I met him and your grandfather, Old Jobey. I never took a shine to him, but your father was very different."

"I never knew him, sir," said AJ. "What was he like?"

"I remember him as a handsome man with an eye for the ladies—or rather, an eye for one particular lady. Your mother was a lovely young woman, full of hope, and Lucas Jobey was determined to marry her, despite, I believe, some family difficulties."

"It never happened," said AJ.

"Oh, the marriage went ahead, all right. I remember that Baldwin attended the ceremony."

"So I'm not a bastard, then—sir?"

"Not in any legal sense."

"Bloody hell," said AJ quietly.

They were just outside 4 Raymond Buildings when Mr. Groat's mobile rang.

"Where is the blasted thing?" said Mr. Groat, fumbling in his briefcase. "Hello? Yes." There was a long pause before Mr. Groat said, "When?" He reached out and held on to the railings. "Thank you," he said and ended the call.

AJ took the phone and put it back in the briefcase. Mr. Groat was gazing into a vague and distant place.

"Has something happened, sir?" AJ asked.

"In a word, yes. Mr. Baldwin died an hour ago."

CHAPTER 18

The wheezy sound of a vacuum cleaner acted as an alarm for AJ. Elsie was always up at six, and she liked to hoover before switching on the radio to listen to the international disasters, as she called them. AJ crawled out of bed. He had hoped to see the professor before he went back through the door, but there was no time. The consequences of Mr. Baldwin's murder were taking up nearly every minute that could be squeezed from a day.

"I'm off to work," he told Elsie when he was dressed. "Then I'm going away for the weekend with Slim."

"Where to?" she asked.

"Nowhere special." AJ felt his cheeks go red. He wished he was better at lying. "Slim's a bit down after his breakup with Sicknote."

"You're a good friend, you are," said Elsie. "But when you come back, maybe you should go and see your mum. Jan was down here yesterday in tears. She said to me she'd made a right royal mess of things." Elsie lowered her voice, as if Jan might have her ear glued to Elsie's front door. "She said the Slug had moved out."

"I will," said AJ. "On Monday."

He closed the front door and for a moment tried to imagine his mum having any regrets at all. In the dim morning light the concrete steps of the stairwell sparkled. When he was a little lad he had believed he and his mum were rich because the stairs had diamonds in them. He could hear Jan shouting at Roxy. Things must be bad.

It was still early when he arrived at Raymond Buildings. He would have to wait until the doors were unlocked. He stood on the step and checked his messages. All were from Slim, who sounded more worried with every text he sent. AJ texted him back.

"calm it armit," he wrote. "cu at 6."

He waited in the rain, regretting that he didn't own a proper winter coat. The one thought that kept him warm was the release that Mr. Baldwin's death had brought about. The weight of a mountain had been taken from his shoulders. Although if—and it was a big if—he could find the documentation it would help Ms. Finch win the case. And it wouldn't do his prospects any harm either.

AJ was now so wet that he rang the bell on the off chance that one of the cleaners might still be there. To his surprise, Morton's voice snapped down the entry phone.

"It's me, Aiden," said AJ.

"Stay there."

AJ watched through the glass as Morton came down the stairs.

"Good morning," AJ said.

"Is it?" said Morton. "I hadn't noticed."

It occurred to AJ that Morton hadn't been home.

"Are you squeamish?" Morton asked him.

"No. I don't think so," said AJ.

"Come on. There is someone I need to see."

That was all the explanation AJ was given.

Morton was no more forthcoming when their taxi drew up at an impersonal office building, and AJ felt it would be a mistake to ask any questions. A lift took them to the basement, where the door opened with a judder and the low light made it feel as if they were in a submarine. A man in a white coat appeared in the corridor. He had a face divided by a bridge of eyebrows that ran as straight as Roman Road and overshadowed his eyes.

"This is very good of you, Ron," said Morton, shaking his hand. "I owe you one."

The man pushed open a door on which was a nameplate that read:

R E Haggerty
Senior Forensic Pathologist

"And this is?" said the man, looking at AJ, the drawbridge of his eyebrows rising.

"Aiden, a baby clerk," said Morton.

AJ stood up a little straighter.

"So, Aiden," said Mr. Haggerty. "You are one of the chosen few. You must be a bright lad."

The room was clinically bare apart from a long white table.

"Take a seat," said Mr. Haggerty.

The chairs scraped across the floor as Morton and AJ pulled them out, the same sound as the chairs at school used to make.

AJ sat down. Through the open door to the next room he could see on a trolley a figure covered in a cloth, a toe sticking out, white and waxy. With a shock he realized he was looking at the corpse of Mr. Baldwin.

"This is an intriguing case," said Mr. Haggerty. "These are, of course, only the initial findings. More work needs to be done."

Morton nodded.

Mr. Haggerty collected two files and put them before him; then, staring at no one in particular, started.

"The postmortem shows that Mr. Baldwin swallowed arsenic trioxide, known as white arsenic."

"White arsenic?" interrupted Morton. "Wasn't that used in the early nineteenth century? You never hear of it now."

"Yes, they called it the inheritance powder," said Mr. Haggerty. "It was very unpredictable. Some victims were struck down instantly, some died in eleven hours or so and others took two weeks.

"Whoever murdered Mr. Baldwin wanted him to take time dying. I would say the murderer knew what he was doing, even took a perverse delight in killing. One has to ask oneself why, in this day and age, would anyone go to so much trouble?"

"Why indeed?" said Morton. "I gather that what you are about to tell me is not what I want to hear."

"Let's start with the clothes Mr. Baldwin was wearing at the time he was taken ill. His suit was made in Savile Row, his shoes were from Lobbs. But the interesting thing is his scarf. It looks as good as new but in fact was made by Mare Brothers of Clerkenwell Road, who went out of business in 1900. The tailors kept meticulous records, and the Mare family put them online in 2012. The scarf was purchased in December 1826 by a Mr. Dalton."

AJ struggled to arrange his features.

"I suppose his first name wasn't Samuel, by any chance," said Morton.

"Actually, it was," said Mr. Haggerty.

"A coincidence, that's all," said Morton. "Mr. Baldwin was in the middle of a fraud case, and his client swears that he received the snuffboxes in question from a Samuel Dalton. It must be an alias. There's no record of the man ever having existed."

"Except in 1826," said Mr. Haggerty.

"That's no help to us," said Morton, who, unlike AJ, was having trouble taking all this in. "So you're telling me that Mr. Baldwin swallowed arsenic given to him by some nutcase who is keen to enact a nineteenth-century-style murder. Do you think it could be one of his clients with a grudge?"

"It's possible," said Mr. Haggerty. "A client with a grudge and a degree in toxicology. As you may know, I'm writing a book about historic cases of poisoning. One I'm particularly interested in took place early in 1813. To me it's obvious that the perpetrator had studied the effects of poison, as an entire family died within a matter of hours. There was a great deal of interest in it, because the supposed murderer was a seventeen-year-old servant girl. It seems most unlikely that a servant would have an apothecary's knowledge of poisons."

Damn, thought AJ. Hadn't Mr. Stone said that a servant had been accused of murdering the Jobey family?

"When are you showing this report to Detective Poilaine?" said Morton.

"I'm just about to send it over."

"Thanks, Ron," said Morton as they walked towards the lift.

"Mr. Haggerty," said AJ, trying to sound calm. "Where can I find out more about the 1813 murder? Is there anything online?"

"No, there isn't. But if you're interested I'll email my account of it to you."

Once out of the building, Morton checked his emails.

"Better get back to Raymond Buildings in case Detective Poilaine turns up," he said. "Don't say a word to anyone about our visit to Ron Haggerty."

"No, I won't," said AJ.

"Oh, I nearly forgot. This arrived for you," said Morton. He handed AJ a thick envelope and hailed a cab.

AJ waited until he was alone at his desk before he opened the envelope. Inside was a book, small and beautiful, with drawings and maps of London. AJ had never owned anything so old. Tucked in the back was what looked like Monopoly money. It wouldn't buy anything here, thought AJ. Not even a sandwich. There was a note from the professor.

"Things have taken a decidedly awkward turn," it read. "I assume that you will be going back through the door. Be careful. I will see you next week."

AJ put the book and the note in his pocket. His mobile rang.

Slim said, "Can we go any sooner, mate? I can't hang on until this evening." "You'll have to," said AJ.

"I might be dead by then."

"Try not to be."

CHAPTER 19

AJ arrived at Mount Pleasant around six o'clock as planned but there was no sign of Slim. He waited at the corner of Phoenix Place and then started to pace back and forth. He heard a siren in the distance, and images of a beaten-up Slim flickered ambulance-blue across his imagination. What if Moses had found him? Then what? Perhaps waiting until Friday had been a day too long. AJ told himself he had to stop thinking the worst about everything.

Finally, at twenty to seven, AJ got through to Slim on his mobile. He sounded so faint that for a moment AJ wasn't sure if there was anybody at the end of the line.

"Slim—is that you?"

"Yeah."

"Where are you?"

"Homerton Hospital, in A&E." Slim's voice sounded shaky, on the brink of tears. "Moses tried to kill me, man."

"Is anything broken?"

"Just my heart. Sicknote sat in that pimped-up car of his filing her razor-blade fingernails while Moses beat the crap out of me. She did nothing. Nothing." His words stumbled on a choke. "I was saved by a copper. If he hadn't turned up, I think I'd be in the morgue."

"Stay there," said AJ. "I'll pick you up."

"What in? You don't drive."

"Just stay there."

"Moses keeps texting me saying he's waiting outside to kill me."

"I'll be there as fast as I can."

"You're a real friend, bro."

AJ had taken fifty pounds from his savings account. He had planned to give it to Elsie towards the rent. But this was an emergency, and of all the people he knew Elsie would the first to understand why he had to use it. He hailed a cab.

Slim was squashed next to a vending machine, his face an explosion of bruises. His two black eyes were fixed on the sliding door of A&E. He looked more frightened than a rabbit caught short on a motorway.

"Come on," said AJ.

Slim had been given a crutch, and he hobbled in an ungainly manner towards the taxi. The cabbie looked none too pleased.

"If he's drunk," he said bluntly, "I'm not taking him—or you."

"He's just bashed up," said AJ.

Slim sank down as low as he could in the back of the cab. His mobile bleeped.

"Was he out there?" he said.

"Who?" said AJ.

"Moses, who else? That was another text saying I'm dead meat."

"What happened?" asked AJ.

"I was staying with an uncle who has a garage round the back of Hackney Downs. I thought I was pretty safe there because it's nowhere near Moses's manor. Someone must've seen me. Y'know, I don't think Sicknote would give a monkey's if I was dead. Bloody hell. That's a sad thought."

AJ was thinking that he had two problems, and both of them appeared insurmountable. First, how would Slim climb over the fence in the state he was in, and second, what would he do with Slim once they were through the door?

AJ took out the *Useful Hints for Travelers* book the professor had sent him and read.

It is an unconventional rule that the inns most frequented are those whose charges are the most reasonable. We may add that a traveler whose deportment is civil and obliging will always be better served than the rude and overbearing. Wherever one stays nothing is more unwholesome than to sleep in a room that has been a long time shut up. The windows should be opened immediately.

AJ flicked through the book to find what he would be expected to pay. And how far the professor's money might go.

The cab dropped them at the corner of Phoenix Place. In the darkness the car park looked dangerous in a way that only derelict places can.

"Well," said Slim. "What now?"

The news that AJ expected Slim to climb over the fence did not go down well. In a catalog of complaints, all of them were to do with the fact that his bones hurt and that Moses would find him.

"That's called paranoia," said AJ. He wondered how much to tell Slim before he tried to find the door. Seeing the mess he made climbing over the fence he decided to keep quiet.

"I'm not staying here in this car park. That's not the plan, is it?" said Slim. He looked about him desperately. "I bet there's a guard dog here, and if there is it will just go for me—dogs always do. I'll be the dog's dinner. Let's leave now."

"No," said AJ. "It'll be all right, I promise. Just give me a moment to work this out."

"Work what out? We're in a deserted car park with lights all round it, so whoever breaks into the car park can be seen. And no doubt we're being recorded on CCTV right this minute."

Slim's phone bleeped again.

"What're we doing here?" said Slim. "It's bloody freezing."

AJ took out his mobile phone in order to see better. In its beam he saw the dead growth that looked like the face of the devil.

Slim was decidedly miserable.

"If you think you're going to hide me here you've got another think coming. This place is dead spooky. I want to go." In the distance they heard barking. "Oh no, that's all we need," said Slim. "I told you there were guard dogs."

"Hey, you!" came a voice. "This is private property. It belongs to the Royal Mail. You shouldn't be here. You're trespassing."

"Great," said Slim. "I wait all week, believing you can save me, only to be taken to a skanky car park where we're going to be arrested and thrown into the jug. I won't be any safer there than out on the streets."

"Be quiet," said AJ. He could see the security guard a way off.

"I'm calling the police!" the guard shouted.

As the guard began to stride towards them the fog rose, and with it the stink of the River Fleet.

"Quick."

Slim looked at him as if he was deranged.

"You gone mad?" he said.

"No—just do as I tell you. We don't have much time."

Slim, resigned to a fate unknown, did as he was told.

"Hold on to me," said AJ, helping him up.

He could hear Slim's teeth chattering, the bleep of his phone. He could hear the security guard in the fog, the whirl of the police sirens.

And then, just when he thought it was too late, that maybe he had imagined the door, the house, the whole kaboodle, there it was. Never had AJ been so pleased to see anything as he was to see Jobey's Door.

CHAPTER 20

"It worked, Slim, it worked," said AJ, a huge grin on his face.

They were standing in the ill-lit hall.

"Where are we?" said Slim. "This is beyond weird. I never saw a house in the car park."

"You know the best thing about being here?" said AJ.

"What?"

"Moses will never find you."

"How do you make that out? Moses is just as likely to find me here as anywhere else."

He took out his phone, stared at it and pressed all its buttons.

"There's no reception," he said, shaking it. "Where are we? In the Stone Age?"

"The nineteenth century."

"I know you mean well, bro," said Slim, "but this place really gives me the creeps. It feels like a joint ghosts might hang out in." There was a sound from upstairs and he backed towards the door. A face lit by a single candle peered over the banisters. "See? I told you. A ghost."

"Mr. Jobey," said Ingleby, coming down the stairs, his boots leaving footprints in the dust. "Back again. And who might this young man be?"

"A friend of mine."

"A friend of yours. Are you intending to bring all your friends here?"

"No, Mr. Ingleby. Only the ones in trouble."

"Many, are they?"

"Two."

"And are you going to introduce me?"

"This is Slim. Slim, this is Mr. Ingleby."

Slim looked quite bewildered. He'd never seen anyone dressed like the man standing before him, except on TV.

Ingleby went to the cupboard where AJ had left his clothes and unlocked a small door and pulled out a basket.

"I will take the modern-day accoutrements from you."

"The what?" said Slim.

Ingleby held out the basket and shook it.

"I don't have any money, if that's what you want," said Slim.

"Give him your mobile and anything synthetic, including your trainers," hissed AJ.

"Why would I want to do that? My mobile is my lifeline, my trainers are priceless."

"Not here, they're not," said AJ, putting his own phone and the brogues that were two sizes too big in the basket.

Reluctantly Slim handed over his mobile and shoes and finally let go of his crutch.

"What's all this in aid of?" he asked. "That crutch belongs to the National Health Science."

Ingleby said not a word as he locked them all away. Then, as if he had touched something dirty, he dusted his hands.

"Come, Mr. Slim," he said. "We'll find you clothes more suitable for today's climate."

In his socks, Slim hobbled upstairs after Ingleby. AJ put on the clothes that he'd left there. When Slim reappeared AJ was surprised by how good he looked. Being lanky, he had always appeared a little scrawny, but these clothes padded him out and gave him an air of elegance. Even with two black eyes you could tell he was a man about town.

He whispered to AJ, "Moses would never touch a toff such as I, would he?" Then, seeing that Ingleby intended to take them out the front door, said, "You know the Old Bill are out there with dogs? And they are waiting for us."

"I doubt it," said Ingleby.

The door opened onto a different world and, as far as Slim was concerned, a different planet.

"Where the hell are we?"

"The great and terrible metropolis of London, a world unto itself," said Ingelby, hailing a hackney cab. "Fetter Lane," he said, opening the door.

Outside, the fog had gathered its forces and was now so thick that only a globe of lamplight gave any indication as to where the road ended and the pavement began. Horses, carts and people appeared out of the fog to disappear almost at once.

"Bloody hell," said Slim. "This must be costing a fortune—the fog, the sets, the scenery. I wonder what they're filming."

"They're not filming anything," said AJ.

"What's going on, then?"

Ingleby answered.

"Mr. Slim, you and your friend Mr. Jobey are time travelers."

"You're not serious? I mean, that's a joke, right?" said Slim.

"No," said Ingleby. "And the first rule of time travel is that you never—and I mean never—whisper a word to anyone about the future."

The hackney cab pulled up outside a boardinghouse. Ingleby had explained on the journey that it was run by a Mrs. Furby, who was a widow and sadly had never found herself another husband. AJ had imagined Mrs. Furby to be old and, by the surprise on his face when they were greeted in the hall by an attractive woman in her early twenties, so had Slim.

"You're very welcome," she said, taking them all into the parlor.

"These are two travelers who have just arrived in London," explained Ingleby. "They have good money and are trustworthy gents."

"Honored, I am sure. I like to think that I keep a regular and clean house, with honest and God-fearing boarders."

Slim looked completely done in. His face was white, his bruises multiple shades of blue and purple. Mrs. Furby turned up the oil lamp and put her hands to her mouth at the sight of him. An expression of horror came over her face.

"The world is a pretty kettle of fish," she said, "when a foreigner is accosted on his way to this great city." She paused for a moment and then said, "Highwaymen?" but before Ingleby could answer she had already concluded that Slim must have fought them off and that the rogues were no doubt lying in a ditch. Slim was quite lost for words, and his silence convinced her that she was right. "And you traveled all the way from Italy?"

AJ interrupted before Slim could say, no, Stoke Newington.

"No, he's of Turkish origin."

"Turkish?" she said. She showed them to the top of the house and opened a door to a set of rooms: two bedrooms and a small parlor, sparsely furnished but as clean as a whistle. "I hope this is to your satisfaction."

"Where's the—"

AJ kicked Slim, who was on the verge of asking where the bog was.

"Yes," said AJ. "It's perfect, thank you."

Ingleby left, saying he would return tomorrow.

There were three other boarders in the house: a widow and her daughter, a plain girl who had little to say, and a man who announced himself as Mr. Flint, who did not appear to be a bright spark. The food, though, was excellent, and the conversation was led by Mrs. Furby, who made up for the quietness of her guests.

"My father went to Constantinople, Mr. Slim," said Mrs. Furby, handing him a plate of steak and kidney pudding. "He died at Waterloo."

Slim opened his mouth to comment, but AJ kicked him again and he said nothing.

"It isn't called Constantinople anymore," said Slim when they were alone in their rooms. "She should have said Istanbul. And how did her father come to die at Waterloo? Do you think he was pushed onto the rails? Or maybe committed suicide?"

"She wasn't talking about the station, she was talking about the Battle of Waterloo. You know, the Duke of Wellington and Napoleon and all that."

"Hell," said Slim. "I wish I'd paid more attention to geography and history. Especially history."

"Tomorrow," said AJ, taking off his jacket, "I need to see someone."

"Who?" said Slim.

AJ chose not to answer the question. He planned to pay another visit to Miss Esme. He felt that now he and Miss Esme knew each other a little better, he could bring up the subject of the papers on his next visit. He wasn't sure quite how to go about it without a phone. He couldn't just turn up on her doorstep again. It wasn't, he knew, the correct thing to do.

"What are you doing?" Slim asked.

"Writing a message."

"Who to?"

"No one you know. Now, listen, I need you to find out how much this money is worth, what it'll buy."

He gave Slim the notes the professor had sent him. "Don't let anyone cheat you out of it."

"Cheat *me*?" said Slim indignantly. "I haven't spent two years working in Dalston Market without learning something."

CHAPTER 21

AJ had the next day planned and the note was in his pocket ready to be delivered.

"Are you going to be OK?" AJ said to Slim.

"Don't you worry about me," said Slim. "I'm raring to go."

"That is exactly what I'm worried about," said AJ, laughing.

Downstairs AJ found Ingleby waiting for him in the parlor.

"There is someone I want you to meet," said Ingleby.

AJ was about to protest, but the look on Ingleby's face was adamant. He knew it would be hopeless. Mrs. Furby said she would see that the note was delivered.

Ingleby firmly took AJ's arm and strode off in the direction of Holborn.

"Not Mr. Stone?" said AJ, slowing down. "Are you going to tell me all over again that I should lock the door and piss off? Or what? I'll end up garrotted in a ditch?"

"Don't be ridiculous. And this is nothing at all to do with Mr. Stone," said Ingleby. "The man you are to meet has spent many years abroad. Now, I need to concentrate."

"On what?"

"On making sure, sir, that no one has taken the liberty of

following us. I need to keep my wits about me and not be bamboozled by questions."

Near the River Fleet at Farringdon, the houses were wooden, grown tall not by design but by necessity. It was a place that AJ, streetwise as he was, would not have cared to visit at night. They crossed a small bridge where the river stagnated under ice. Even in the bitter cold its shit-filled perfume hung heavy in the air. In a narrow street that backed onto the water, Ingleby once more looked quickly about him and stopped at an inn that no architect would have claimed having had a hand in. If anyone from the local council clapped eyes on the place, thought AJ, they would have the whole kaboodle pulled down on the grounds of health and safety. Four ragamuffins rushed up to AJ with their hands out.

"Bugger off, all of you," said Ingleby.

AJ felt that at any moment the Artful Dodger would come swaggering along and Fagin's face might appear from an attic window. Instead the door was opened by a rodent of a man, who peered round it, nose twitching, dark eyes glittering this way and that. AJ was reminded of Dr. Jinx.

"Any clingers? Anyone hiding in the shadows of your footsteps?"

"No. Now let us in," snapped Ingleby.

They were shown into a rat hole and up three flights of stairs, along more passages and into a chamber with a bow window that leaned over the river. It was colder in the room than it was outside, and the only light seemed to come from the whiteness of a linen tablecloth. On it had been placed a piping-hot pie, a loaf of bread, a jug of wine and plates and cutlery for three.

The rat stood still as a door stopper.

"Silence is expensive," he said.

Ingleby turned on him and put both his hands round the neck of the astonished rat.

"If one foul breath of yours whispers even a word of this to anyone then you will be thrown by me into the Fleet, and may the vermin feast off you."

The rat shook himself free.

"I meant no offense," said the rat, pulling at his neck scarf. "My tongue is a lead weight when it comes to the matter of words better not said."

"I'm glad to hear it," said Ingleby, and pressed some coins into his hand. "If only for your sake."

The rat scurried away.

AJ couldn't think why Ingleby would want to visit such a grim place and waited for an explanation, but Ingleby stood as if expecting something to happen, eyeing the pie with longing. It was, after all, the warmest thing the room had to offer.

"A pity to let a pie of such noble proportions go cold," said Ingleby at last.

"Too right, mate."

AJ jumped. The voice came from under the floorboards. Ingleby quickly rolled back the threadbare rug and lifted a trapdoor, whereupon a man's head appeared, and with a swift movement the man heaved himself up. He stood before them with a smile neither sincere nor insincere, its purpose more a mask to hide his grief. He studied AJ, hummed to himself as if confirming all he thought, then sat down and helped himself to a slice of pie.

Without a moment's hesitation Ingleby joined him and tucked in with real appetite, helping them both to wine and tearing off chunks of bread.

AJ thought he could be looking at a picture in a museum portraying two villains eating a dainty pie.

"Who are you?" asked AJ.

The man, his mouth full of hot pie, splattered, "I've got no name." He paused. "You can call me Nonsuch, if you like."

"Why won't you tell me your name?" asked AJ. "What's in it that makes it so bad?"

The man who called himself Nonsuch said, "You're the dead spit of your father."

"You knew him?"

"Knew him? He was my best mate. He's the reason I'm here."

"How did you know him?" he asked.

"I'll tell you when the time's right. What you don't know won't kill you. Relax, have some pie." AJ sat down at the table. "I want you to do something for me. Something I can't do and neither can Ingleby."

"Why's that?"

Nonsuch had a knack of ignoring questions he didn't want to answer.

"Let's put it like this. I've been out of the country doing time, and now that I'm back, there are certain persons who I would prefer not to have my address, if you get my drift." He wiped his mouth on the tablecloth. "Shall we just concentrate on the present?"

"A word with too many definitions for my liking," said AJ.

"It's simple," said Nonsuch. "What I want you to do is bring Esme to me."

"Esme Dalton?" said AJ. "You must be joking. Look, you seem a good sort of geezer. I don't know what you've done or how you knew my father. All I do know is that none of what you're saying makes any sense."

"Don't worry about it. Ingleby will tell you where and when. Just don't leave it too long. I don't have time or the law on my side and I want to see Esme . . . I want to see my daughter once before it's too late."

CHAPTER 22

Slim had a fire blazing in their rooms and was sitting in an armchair that hadn't been there that morning.

"What have you been up to?" asked AJ, genuinely shocked.

"Bought a few things, bro, to make us comfortable. Mrs. Furby told me where to go, who to do business with and who to leave well alone." He paused. "Do you like it? It feels more homely." AJ was gobsmacked. "I've never had a room of my own," said Slim. "I've always had to share. This is a first. Oh—this came for you."

Written on a gold-edged card was an invitation to call for afternoon tea at the Dalton house at four o'clock the following afternoon. AJ smiled.

There was a knock on the door. Slim leapt up as two panting men carried in another armchair.

"Just there," said Slim with authority. The men stood by the door, waiting, and he gave them a coin for their trouble.

"We don't need all this," said AJ. "We're not going to stay here—it's just until things have cooled down back home. Anyway, what are we going to do once that money's gone?"

"That money, bro, is enough for two gents to live off like

lords for a year, and I've got a plan to make it go even further." He took from his pocket two snuffboxes. "They cost nothing, and look at them—I'm telling you I could flog these for a small fortune back home."

AJ sat down, comfortably defeated.

"Slim," he said. "When I go back I'll see what the situation is with Moses, and if everything's calmed down I'll come for you next weekend."

"Hold on—not so fast," said Slim. "I've had the best day of my life here. I mean, I miss having a bog that you can flush, but that aside, this is a pretty cool place to be. I just have to make sure no one diddles us with fake notes, because when you look at them they are pretty easy to forge, and apparently it's done quite a lot. So Mrs. Furby tells me. I walked through the city and thought, What a bloody mess we made of London. Why did we knock down so many beautiful buildings?" He stopped, poked the fire and poured a glass of beer from a jug. "Want some?" AJ nodded and Slim poured another. "The plan is this. You take these snuffboxes back, flog them and change the money into gold."

"Great," said AJ. "And get arrested on suspicion of dealing in stolen property—or fake goods."

AJ couldn't remember when he'd last seen Slim this happy.

"I've thought that one through," said Slim. "My uncle Nazif, the one who mends cars near Hackney Downs, knows this geezer who deals in antiques, all aboveboard, no questions asked. Here, I've written down the address."

"Aren't you itching to go back to the time you know?"

"Why in hell would I? No smug, preening tossers who think

anything lower than an A* grade means your life is over. No mobile, no Facebook, no way for Sicknote to torment me. I'm fine here—no one will miss me, and Moses can't kill me."

"I thought Sicknote was the love of your life."

"She's history," said Slim. "She hasn't any culture. Not like Mrs. Furby."

AJ burst out laughing.

"Plenty more fish in the sea, then?"

"You could say that. I've been thinking," said Slim. "You should bring Leon here. He could do with his life being reset too."

"Maybe—if I can find him," said AJ. "And if he would want to come."

"He will," said Slim. "I know it."

Slim's enthusiasm was infectious. Yes, thought AJ. He could see all three of them together here.

That night they again ate supper with Mrs. Furby, who had taken a shine to Slim. AJ let the conversation run over him while he thought about Miss Esme. He couldn't wait to see her again. He'd never been like this about a girl before. Certainly not about Alice, his first girlfriend.

"Will you be coming with us to visit St. Paul's tomorrow, Mr. Jobey?" asked Mrs. Furby.

"Of course he will," said Slim, who as far as AJ knew had never in his whole life been inside a church, let alone a cathedral. Or a mosque, for that matter.

"I can't tomorrow," said AJ. "I've been invited to call on Miss Esme Dalton."

"Oh, what fine friends you have, Mr. Jobey," said Mrs. Furby.

"I'm not quite up on the etiquette of polite society," said AJ, "and I was wondering . . ."

Mrs. Furby clapped her hands together with delight.

"Why, I have just bought two books on the subject. They are becoming most popular. You must borrow them, Mr. Jobey, and anything else that might help. I hope you will be back to dine with us tomorrow night. I like my house to be full of lively people."

AJ looked at Mr. Flint, who hadn't said a word, and the widow and daughter, who were equally quiet, and knew exactly why Mrs. Furby enjoyed Slim's company.

The next day arrived to the sound of bells hammering out over London. One thing was for sure, no one could sleep through it unless they were stone deaf. The chamber shuddered with the noise.

Slim was already up and dressed.

"Where're you going?" asked AJ.

"To see St. Paul's, remember?" said Slim.

"Since when have you been interested in sightseeing?"

"When in Rome," said Slim, "do as the Romans."

Mrs. Furby said again how sorry she was that AJ couldn't join them. Slim told her that, anyway, AJ belonged to a different kind of congregation. "Don't you?"

"Ye-es," said AJ uncertainly.

"The Church of the Anaesthetists," said Slim.

Mrs. Furby had never heard of it before. Slim winked at AJ and said he would tell her about it on the way to St. Paul's.

AJ watched Slim and Mrs. Furby walk together down the street, Slim holding forth about some crazy religious stuff that no one in that century or any other century had ever heard before.

AJ went back to his room with the books Mrs. Furby had lent him. In the first one he read:

BASIC SOCIAL RULES FOR GENTLEMEN
- *Stare in no one's face.*
- *Eat not fast nor slow.*
- *Smell not your meat when eating.*
- *Spit not onto the carpet.*
- *Offer not another your handkerchief.*
- *Always wear gloves on the street, in church & at other formal occasions, except when eating or drinking. White or cream-colored gloves for evening, gray or other darker colors for day wear.*
- *Remove your hat when entering a building.*
- *Stand up when a lady enters a room.*

AJ wasn't sure he would ever master 1830s etiquette. It seemed so pointless. The second book was on social rules for ladies. It was shocking. As far as he could make out, ladies weren't allowed to read books or go to the theater. Even Shakespeare was thought to be too much for their frail constitutions to bear. When he reached the part about how a lady must always be corseted he wondered why there hadn't been a mass rebellion. He thought of Miss Esme. She was so skinny, there was surely

nothing to corset; and as for always being chaperoned, well, he'd only met her twice, and on both occasions she wasn't.

According to this set of rules she had blown her chances in the marriage cattle market.

This is stupid, thought AJ. But better buy some gloves, just in case.

CHAPTER 23

AJ wondered if Clerkenwell Green had ever been green. The houses surrounding it and the church all looked pretty enough, but quite where green came in he didn't know. Several hens had escaped from a backyard and were being chased by a boy with a stick; horses clip-clopped past. Most people seemed to walk with a purpose. AJ, being early, dawdled, looking in the shops. One caught his fancy. It sold nothing but birds. A raven stood in a cage, pecking at the bars; there were singing canaries, even a nightingale, and in a dark corner were two magpies. The shop owner perched on a stool, covered in white dust, looking as if all he was missing was his feathers.

"Are they all for sale?" AJ asked him.

"Every single one of them," he said. "All trained, all as polite as a bird can be."

The church clock struck a quarter to four and it was already dark, the streets emptying of people, with only dim lamps lighting the way. When he returned to Mrs. Furby's, he decided, he would treat himself to a hackney carriage.

He hoped that he might be able to see Miss Esme alone, although, according to the book on manners, such a meeting was out of the question. He didn't fancy telling Miss Esme about Nonsuch in Mrs. Meacock's presence.

He knocked on the Daltons' door, feeling more nervous than he thought he should.

A manservant let him in and said that Mrs. Meacock wasn't yet home. AJ handed over his hat, coat and muffler but wasn't sure if he should keep the gray leather gloves, especially as he'd gone to all the trouble of buying them. Shouldn't he at least show them off? The manservant was impatient, and reluctantly AJ let him take the gloves as well. The house was bitterly cold, and he was surprised to find he could see his breath indoors more clearly than he could outside.

"Mr. Jobey."

He looked up. Miss Esme stood on the stairs, wearing a black dress more stylish than anything she had worn before.

"Please come up and warm yourself," she said.

The drawing room felt like a mausoleum.

Miss Esme stood by the fire.

"I'm afraid I'm early," AJ said. "I wanted to see you alone."

She blushed. He hadn't seen a girl blush like that since Year Nine, when Kiely Scott's knickers fell down in the playground.

AJ felt awkward. All the easy conversation of their last meeting had gone. The house felt as heavy as nightmares—not a place AJ wanted to stay in long. The drawing room was oppressive; the furniture judgmental; the mantelpiece, the pictures, the ornaments overbearing. It appeared to him that at any moment Miss Esme would be crushed by their weight.

He was at a loss as to what to say. The tick of the clock seemed to swallow all possible topics of conversation. There was an uncomfortable silence; it was as if they hardly knew one another.

"Is your mother in?" he asked.

"My mother? She died in a madhouse. My father was quite sure I too would end up there."

"Why? You seem perfectly sane to me," said AJ. "What sent your mother mad?"

"My father," she said quietly. "Of that I have always been certain." She hesitated. "My mother worked to help the women prisoners who were brought to trial at the Old Bailey. My father believed that Newgate Prison was the cause of her malady. Ten years ago they took her away. I wasn't allowed to see her again. Three years later she died."

What AJ would have given to be able to talk to her as he had before, without all the jagged edges of etiquette.

"I don't know what to say. I'm a traveler—I haven't got the right language."

"You have more honesty and understanding than many others."

Feeling bolder, AJ said, "Can I ask you a question? Were you ever close to your father?"

The light went out of her face.

Her voice tightened. "No, never. What makes you ask?"

Because, thought AJ, I've just met an ex-con who claims to be your real dad.

Human beings are basically all the same, it's only the gadgets that have changed. His world was cluttered with emails, texts and mobile phones. And still, he thought, we don't know how to communicate.

"I shouldn't have come so early," he said.

"Will you sit?" she said.

AJ sat.

"My father's death was put down to an infection."

"Not poison, as you thought?" said AJ.

She shook her head.

"When my father's will was read, I found out that I had inherited his estate, but if I were to go mad or die before I married then the estate would go to Mrs. Meacock."

"You remember the lawyer, Mr. Baldwin," said AJ. "You said he helped your father with the will."

"Yes," she said. "Why he advised my father to frame his will as he did, I wish I knew."

"Mr. Baldwin died three days ago of arsenic poisoning."

All the color in her face drained away.

"Another one, then," she said.

She was about to say more when outside the room a stair creaked. AJ hadn't lived with his mother for seventeen years without knowing when someone's ear was firmly embedded in a door. He put his finger to his lips.

"It's much colder here than in my city," he said, and moved quietly to the door.

He opened it so suddenly that Mrs. Meacock tumbled into the room. AJ helped her to her feet.

"Oh dear, oh dear," she said, her voice flavored with artificial sweeteners. She was a small woman with a righteous air about her to disguise her nosiness. AJ noticed that Miss Esme moved quickly away from her. "And here you are, Mr. Jobey. It is a pleasure to see you again. Poor Miss Esme has been through such a terrible time, haven't you, my dear, that you quite forgot that you should be chaperoned when a gentleman pays a visit. It is just us, Mr. Jobey. I hope you don't mind, but we are in mourning."

"I understand," said AJ.

Mrs. Meacock seated herself, making a play of her skirts and reminding AJ of a cartoon hen sat upon an egg.

They talked, or rather Mrs. Meacock talked, and made long sentences into small talk until a tray of tea was served, accompanied by a decanter of wine with one glass. AJ smiled to himself, imagining what Mrs. Meacock might make of TV suppers. She poured the tea, still talking. AJ wondered if she ever stopped talking.

He had just succeeded in balancing his cup and saucer and his plate of sandwiches when Mrs. Meacock said to Miss Esme, "Why, my dear, I have only just noticed that you aren't wearing the necklace that I left out on your dressing table."

Instinctively, Miss Esme's hand went to her throat as if she supposed it might be there.

"I couldn't find it," she said.

Mrs. Meacock laughed.

"Nonsense, my dear. That is not possible. I put it on your dressing table, you saw me do it—remember?"

Miss Esme looked down at her tea cup.

"My dear, do not upset yourself unnecessarily. I am sure it is easily found."

AJ felt he should say something.

"You look fab with or without a necklace," he said, and then felt a right idiot.

"That isn't the point," said Mrs. Meacock, her sweetness flavored with lemon.

She rang the bell and the manservant returned. Mrs. Meacock asked him to send Miss Esme's maid to look for a necklace on her mistress's dressing table.

AJ couldn't work out why she was making such a fuss.

"Oh, forgive me, Mr. Jobey," she said. "Please have some Madeira wine."

She poured him a glass.

"Is no one else drinking?" AJ asked.

"No, I took the pledge. And wine is not good for Miss Esme's constitution. Mr. Dalton kept a very fine wine cellar."

AJ was about to take a sip and then thought perhaps this might be a good time to ask about her late master.

"It was strange that Mr. Dalton should have mistaken me for someone else," said AJ.

"Oh, I have seen it happen to many a dying soul," said Mrs. Meacock. "When they're nearing the end they think they see ghosts. I like to think of them as angels waiting to take them to a far better place."

AJ knew one thing: it was no angel Mr. Dalton had thought he'd seen before he conked it.

A maid came into the room and handed Mrs. Meacock a necklace.

"Where did you find it, Agnes?" she asked.

"On Miss Dalton's dressing table, madam, just where you said."

The maid was dismissed. Mrs. Meacock stood and went to fasten it round Miss Esme's neck. AJ saw her flinch.

"How do you find the Madeira, Mr. Jobey?" Mrs. Meacock asked.

"Oh," said AJ, picking up the glass again. He was about to drink when Miss Esme reached across and knocked the glass from his hand.

"I am sorry," she said. "So sorry. You shouldn't have come here. You should stay away."

And before he could think what to say, she had fled the room.

"Oh dear," said Mrs. Meacock. "And there was I thinking it would be such a pleasant distraction for her to have a visitor. It is very sad, Mr. Jobey. She was always a sensitive child and, alas, her father's death has unsettled her state of mind."

"I should be going," said AJ.

"No, no," insisted Mrs. Meacock. "At least have some Madeira."

"No, thank you. I am expected for dinner."

Outside on St. John Street there wasn't a hackney cab to be seen. He was about to walk away when he looked up at the house and saw Miss Esme in one of the windows, her hand pressed against the glass. She seemed to be waving at him, although he wondered if she wasn't calling for help.

Slim was looking very pleased with himself when AJ returned to Mrs. Furby's. He'd spent an hour playing cards with Mr. Flint and had won handsomely. He was full of his success, and Mrs. Furby had been delighted by his generosity, for he'd refused in the end to take a penny from Mr. Flint.

"You know, she called me a real gentleman. How about that?"

But AJ was lost in his thoughts. Ever since he'd left the Dalton house he'd been going over and over all the things that

Miss Esme had said to him. He felt as if he had met two different Esmes, one full of life and questions, the other imprisoned in herself. Was it possible that this other Esme hated her father enough to have poisoned him—and Mr. Baldwin as well? Then there was Mrs. Meacock: she was more than a bit weird. What was all that nonsense about the necklace? And why had Miss Esme knocked the glass from his hand? There were too many questions and a shortage of answers.

"What's up, bro?" said Slim.

"You haven't asked how I came to know about the door."

"No," said Slim. "I reckoned you'd tell me in your own good time.

"I think a good time might be now," said AJ.

CHAPTER 24

On Monday morning, Morton was deep in a series of meetings with Mr. Groat.

"Something big's going down," said Stephen.

AJ was looking at his emails in the hope that Leon might have contacted him. Much to his surprise, there was an email from Mr. Haggerty.

He pulled his chair closer and clicked on the attachment. The past crashed into him with such a jolt that he felt he had whiplash.

>**Annie Sorrell Executed for the Murder by Poison of the Jobey Family.**
>
>The case of this unfortunate young woman is still a mystery. The question of her innocence or guilt divided public opinion at the time.
>
>Annie Sorrell was an uneducated seventeen-year-old servant girl with, by all contemporary accounts, a natural intelligence. She was tall and handsome and had a cheerful disposition. At the time of the murders

she was engaged to a young man to whom she appeared to have been sincerely attached.

The murder of the Jobey family took place on Saturday, 13th February 1813, at their country house in rural Colney Hatch Lane, north of London. Old Jobey, as he was known, and his wife had one daughter. The Jobeys' only surviving son, Lucas, was born seven years after the death of his last sibling. By all accounts the boy was everything his father had wanted. He was educated at Westminster and went up to Cambridge, where he had shown an interest in the law. But Old Jobey was keen for him to inherit the family business, and Lucas Jobey traveled extensively on his father's behalf.

It was on Lucas's return from one of these journeys that Old Jobey's health began to deteriorate. He had bouts of temper that were completely out of character, and his doctor suggested rest and less meat in the diet.

Mr. Ingleby, who was employed as a secretary in Old Jobey's service, said in his evidence at the inquest that at the beginning of that fateful week his master had not been sleeping well. He refused to take the drafts the doctor gave him, calling them poison. Every night he would check, then check again that all the doors were locked. On the Friday he summoned the family to meet the following day on a matter of urgency.

At the house that Saturday was Old Jobey, his wife, their son Lucas and his sister, Rosamund.

Old Jobey gave the servants the day off. He was a very private man and did not want sensitive family business overheard by anyone. His wife protested, surprised that not even his trusted secretary Ingleby was to remain. Finally, Old Jobey agreed that Annie Sorrell should be left to serve the midday meal.

Annie Sorrell had been with the family two years.

In her testament she said that she had heated the mushroom soup as instructed by Cook and had tasted it with no ill effects. She had left it for a moment to answer the front-door bell, but when she went upstairs there was nobody there.

On returning to the kitchen she poured the soup into a tureen and took it up to the dining room, where the family was deep in conversation. She overheard that Lucas Jobey had recently married and intended to live abroad. She left the soup on the table and went to fetch the pies and cold meats. When she returned, her master was in a furious mood. Her mistress looked frightened and told Annie she would not be needed for the rest of the day.

Annie Sorrell was in the kitchen when the bell to her mistress's bedroom rang. She went up the stairs, past the dining room, where she heard raised voices, and on up to her mistress's room. Annie Sorrell said she found it empty save for a magpie.

She claimed to remember nothing further and concluded that she had fainted. When she came to it was twilight.

She looked round the bedroom and thought she must have dreamt the magpie, for there was no sign of the bird. She lit a candle and made her way downstairs, wondering why no one had called for her. Old Jobey was insistent that the candles be lit at dusk. She noted the time on the hall clock as being half-past five and hurried into the dining room to clear away the dishes before Mr. Ingleby and the servants returned at six o'clock. In her testament she said that she heard a rattling, chattering sound and as she opened the door she felt truly afraid, but it was nothing to what followed.

The family were slumped over the table. All were dead. The tablecloth and rugs were stained with vomit and blood, and strutting about the table was the magpie. Annie Sorrell said she was terrified and ran from the house.

Mr. Ingleby arrived with the servants to find the house in darkness. It was he who discovered the dreadful sight. The kitchen boy was sent to fetch a constable.

The physician who examined the bodies found unmistakeable signs that the victims had been poisoned.

Annie Sorrell was quickly brought to trial, found guilty and sentenced. An eminent lawyer, Mr. Stone of Gray's Inn, went to the judge, offering to produce evidence that proved she could not have committed the crime. The judge assured him that such evidence would be wholly useless and the girl would be hanged in due course.

Annie Sorrell's sentence was delayed until she had

been delivered of the child she was carrying. On the Sunday preceding her execution she was taken to the church inside Newgate Prison, where, in sight of her fellow prisoners, she was seated beside her coffin in the condemned pew inside a black pen. Her face was white, the coffin sharply black, but not one tear did she shed.

The following day a large crowd gathered for her execution, and rooms overlooking the prison courtyard were rented for vast sums of money. Annie Sorrell wore a simple muslin dress, and her last words were "I am innocent."

Her fiancé was present and was so disturbed by the sight of her hanging that he ran amok, attacking officials, and was arrested and brought to trial. He was sentenced to deportation.

AJ scrolled down the document in hope of finding the fiancé's name, but there was nothing more. He stared vacantly into space. Annie Sorrell hovered over him, a leaden angel.

CHAPTER 25

They say travel broadens the mind. If that was the case AJ's mind had expanded to the size of a planet. His brain was a puzzle factory. If Annie Sorrell didn't kill his father, who did? And why? Could Annie Sorrell be Miss Esme's mother? Nonsuch, he knew, was her father, and he'd said that Lucas Jobey was his best mate. It wasn't so far-fetched to conclude that he'd met Annie.

Miss Esme had said that Mrs. Dalton had helped women prisoners in Newgate, and Annie Sorrell's baby was born in Newgate. Yes, he thought, it sort of fitted. And if Mrs. Dalton had taken the baby home to save her from the workhouse, it would go some way to explaining why Samuel Dalton was such a mean monster. Especially if he'd never wanted the child—the child of a convicted murderess. But it was Dalton's will that worried AJ. It was cruel and didn't make any sense.

All miserable families are wasps' nests, AJ thought. Only bees make honey. Next time he went back he would ask Ingleby what else he knew about Annie Sorrell and the murder of the Jobey family.

But before he could return he had to concentrate on finding Leon, and that meant tackling Dr. Jinx. If the past had taught AJ anything, it was not to be frightened of the future.

Dr. Jinx's place of business was a derelict house near the Prince pub. As long as AJ had known the dump it had been covered in scaffolding and plastic—a building site without builders.

Dr. Jinx opened the door and tightened up when he saw AJ. AJ gripped the key in his pocket. The rusty iron gave him courage.

"What the hell do you want?" said Dr. Jinx.

"I'm looking for Leon."

"Awa' an' bile yer heid." Dr. Jinx was about to close the door, but AJ put his foot in it. "I said, wee man, scooby doo."

"When did you last see him?" said AJ.

"Don't make me lose ma rag. Your friend, laddie, is in deep shit. He's taken money that should by rights be mine, and if that little toerag doesn't return it, he'll be dead meat."

AJ pushed his whole body against the door, and to his surprise Jinx let him in. Apart from the stink of skunk, the graffiti-sprayed walls and the electrical sockets, the house could well belong to 1830.

"You're asking for trouble, laddie," said Dr. Jinx.

"No, I'm asking, where is Leon?"

Upstairs, music was playing. AJ could hear laughter, though he couldn't imagine anything funny happening in a dump like this.

"Jinx, baby . . . ," a voice whined from one of the rooms.

Dr. Jinx's mobile rang. He looked at it and turned it off.

"I heard he'd come into some money. The little scrooge bag should ha' paid me back. He should ha' done it because he's upset some very important people and they don't take kindly to anyone taking the cream off the top of their milk."

"So I take it you haven't seen him, then?" said AJ.

"No. If you run into him tell him he's a marked man. Now bugger off and dinna come back."

AJ walked down Edwards Lane, thinking about the deep shit Leon was in and Slim's problem with Moses. He wished he didn't feel so obligated to protect his friends. He was being selfish resenting them, yes, he knew that, but he wanted a chance to find out the truth about his murdered family. Maybe, just maybe, by doing so he would find his own destiny.

If he had been concentrating on the here and now he would have paid more attention to the gang waiting by the gates of Bodman House. In the orange of the streetlight he noticed one of them had a brand-new motorbike. He must have nicked it, thought AJ. Then he saw that in the middle stood Moses.

AJ thought for a moment about turning round. He pulled up his jacket collar, but too late—Moses had seen him. There was nothing for it but to keep walking, avoid eye contact, look like a lion though he felt like a sheep.

"Where he hiding, the goddamn coward?" said Moses. "Where Slim?"

Three of his gang had already blocked the entrance to the flats. A gray cat squeezed past them, meowing.

"How should I know?" said AJ. "I'm not his keeper."

"But you his friend and you know. I see in your eyes, you lying."

One of the gang had Moses's dog, a Staffy, on a chain, and he was not doing a very good job of controlling it.

"Shall I let it go?" he said to Moses.

AJ understood why Slim was so scared of the dog. It looked as if it hadn't been fed for days and was just waiting for a Slim to come along to feast off.

It was then he realized he was surrounded. Over the road he saw Alf from Flat 82 walk past, looking straight ahead. He'd fought in the Second World War, fought for a better country than this—well, that was what he used to tell AJ. He had no more fight in him.

"Give us your mobile," said Moses.

"No," said AJ.

"You give it him now, man, no messin'," said another of Moses's men.

Moses grabbed the phone from AJ before he had even retrieved it from his pocket. He read through the messages.

"See, you lie to me. You seen Slim."

Close up and personal, Moses was a big man. As far as AJ was concerned, he was most probably made of prehistoric bone with a dinosaur of a brain.

"No one lies to Moses," he said, shoving AJ while the rest taunted him.

If this was Moses's game, AJ refused to play. He tried to push past into Bodman House, but Moses grabbed at him.

"You tell Slim, if I see him again I will kill him. I will not forget him. I will kill him for what he done."

"What he's done?" said AJ, making mistake number one and quickly following it with mistake number two. "According to your bird he was incapable of doing anything, so why are you causing so much trouble?"

"No one messes with Moses's girl, no one."

Mistake number three was that AJ didn't stop there even though it was obvious that Moses was out for a fight.

"Slim told me," said AJ, "that you are welcome to her. Sicknote is a goddamn nightmare. It strikes me that you and her are a match made in hell's boudoir."

He saw Moses's face, and something in the glint in his eye had changed. Moses said quietly, "Let the dog go."

AJ hated fighting, had never been that good at it. His stomach did a lurch, and before he even had a chance to raise his fists, Moses had hit him hard on the side of his head. He saw stars, felt himself fighting to stand upright. The third punch felt as if it had a dog attached to it somewhere down in his leg. Then he was lying on the pavement, the dog chewing his arm. Moses's face loomed over him and he pulled AJ up for another round of punches. AJ felt the cold of the pavement hard beneath him again, thought he saw Leon and tried to say, it's all right, bro, stay out of this, but there was too much blood in his mouth. Then everything stopped. He saw trainers running away, smelled petrol from the bike lying abandoned in the road, the fuel running into him. He heard the whining of the dog and he thought, I just need to stand up. It's too cold to lie here.

"He's dead," Alf said.

No, I'm not, AJ wanted to shout. He was shouting, wasn't

he? Don't light a cigarette, Alf, whatever you do, don't light that cigarette. There were more people now.

Someone else said, "Terrible . . ."

I'm alive, thought AJ. What is wrong with everyone? Why couldn't they hear him? The last thing he remembered was blue lights flashing on the inside of his eyelids.

CHAPTER 26

AJ was conscious of lying in bed, tubes coming out of his nose, his mouth, his arms. If I'm dead, he thought, no one would bother with this, would they? He vaguely wondered if it was embalming twenty-first-century style. There was a clinical clank of machinery and the comforting sight of a nurse. She was fiddling with monitors, his bodily functions appearing in ziggly lines.

He drifted in and out of consciousness. At one point he saw his mum. She sat next to him, tears running down her face. Later he wondered if he'd imagined that. Time ran into a sluggish puddle.

"They don't like to keep you in for too long," said Elsie. AJ had been taken from the intensive care unit and put into a side ward. "I would think you'll be out of here before you're ready, dear." She handed him a bag of Brazil nuts. "Hope you don't mind, love, but I sucked the chocolate off them. I washed them afterwards, so they're as good as new."

"Thanks," said AJ, making a mental note not to eat them. "Auntie Elsie, what happened to Moses?"

"Haven't they told you, love? A bloke in a hoodie pushed Moses and his dog off you. They say he probably saved your life. Alf finally collected what's left of his marbles and called the police. Moses ran for it. Not before that dog of his had made a meal of your arm and leg. They arrested Moses an hour later."

"Did they arrest the dog too?"

"It was put down. It was a pit bull cross—it's illegal to own one."

AJ looked at his bandaged arm. A souvenir from a dead dog.

AJ was playing chess with a two-faced man.

"You can't have it both ways," he said. "An open door is an open invitation. I should know. I am Time's bouncer. I keep the riffraff out."

He must have fallen asleep, because when he woke Auntie Elsie had gone. His reality seemed to come in bite sizes, punctuated by the roaring of vivid dreams.

AJ's doctor scanned his chart. AJ tried to sit up. That was a mistake. He couldn't feel his right leg.

"Three broken ribs and concussion," said the doctor.

"Have I still got two legs?"

"Yes. One is rather mauled, but with rest and physiotherapy you should be all right. Where do you live?"

"Bodman House in Stoke Newington."

"Is there a lift?"

"No. That would make life much too easy for everyone."

"Which floor do you live on?"

"The fifth."

"Without a lift?"

AJ nodded. He could see the doctor struggling to imagine what that might be like.

"The police want to ask some questions. Are you up to it?"

"I suppose so," he said, sleep threatening to kidnap him again.

Detective Poilaine must have been waiting outside, as she came in as soon as the doctor had left. AJ hadn't expected to see her. Surely she was too high up to be bothering with a gang beating.

"I'm sorry to see you in such a state, Aiden," she said. "You've had a rough time of it."

He leaned back on the pillows.

"I'm not here about the attack on you—that's being dealt with by Stoke Newington police," said Detective Poilaine. "I am here for an altogether different reason. Last night my colleagues raided premises in Hatton Garden belonging to a fence. He's known to deal in antique jewelry, watches, that sort of thing. Among many other stolen items an extremely-valuable eighteenth-century snuffbox was found. Here, have a look."

She showed him a photo on her mobile phone. He recognized the snuffbox he'd given Leon. A second photo showed an inscription inside the lid. It floated in and out of focus for a moment or two before he was able read it.

Lucas Jobey

———⊷———

Hell.

"It's an unusual surname, Aiden. Was there a Lucas Jobey in your family?"

"I don't know. I'll ask my mum."

"The fence said it had been brought to him about three weeks ago by a young man wearing a hoodie." She sighed. "That description fits nearly all the youths in London. He said he wasn't white."

Please, thought AJ. They haven't arrested Leon. . . .

Something attached to him started to sound alarm bells, and as the nurse rushed in, AJ passed out.

He dreamed he was standing outside a house set among darkly gathered trees. One window was ablaze with light, and through the proscenium arch of the curtains he could see cardboard cutout figures seated at a table. They were his father and his grandfather. On the table a cutout magpie stood, flapping its cardboard wings.

His mum came to visit him and brought Roxy with her. She had made a card with a giant slug on the front. Inside she'd written *Miss You*.

"They said they wouldn't let you out of hospital," Jan said, "because of the stairs and the injury to your leg."

"I don't want to stay here. I am definitely not staying here for Christmas," said AJ.

Jan smiled, and her hard face softened.

"I've told the doctor you'll be staying with Elsie. As she

lives on the second floor and there aren't that many steps, they agreed you could come out tomorrow as long as you rest up."

AJ knew that his mum's pride must have taken a tumble to agree to let him stay at Elsie's.

He did something he'd never done before. He took hold of his mum's hand, and although it hurt him, he squeezed it a little.

Roxy was fiddling about, looking in the bedside locker. Jan took out her purse and gave Roxy some money.

"Go to the shop and buy yourself a bar of chocolate," she said.

AJ waited until she had gone.

"Thanks," he said. "Thanks for coming."

Jan had a tear in her eye.

"Stop it," she said softly. "I don't want to go through an emotional car wash."

The following day he was taken home in an ambulance. Not the kind with flashing lights, but the kind in which rows of ill people sit looking sorry for themselves, and he was definitely one of them. He had been given a walking stick and assured that, with physio, in no time at all he would be as good as new.

Elsie had made a big effort to make the flat look nice and, it being near Christmas, she had even gone so far as to hang up some paper chains. AJ slumped onto her sofa. On the side table sat a purple urn containing Leon's mum's ashes. Elsie had put a little wreath of plastic flowers around the top, and it looked like a strange shrine.

AJ must been staring at it for some time, because when Elsie brought in tea and biscuits she nodded at it and said, "Looks a little brighter, doesn't it? And I'm getting used to the color. I think she quite likes watching TV."

"You are kidding," said AJ, trying not to laugh.

Laughter and broken ribs weren't a good mix.

It was a few days before Christmas Eve when Morton paid a call. AJ, who had taken to watching children's television, mainly because his brain couldn't concentrate on reading, nearly jumped up in surprise when he saw Morton standing there.

"Tea?" said Elsie.

Tea and buttered toast was Elsie's solution to everything that didn't look too serious.

AJ had been dreading this. He knew it was coming. He just wondered why Morton hadn't written to tell him that he was out of a job.

"How're you feeling?" said Morton, handing AJ a well-wrapped package.

"What's this?" asked AJ.

"Open it," said Morton seriously.

Inside AJ found three pork spare ribs.

"I thought you might be needing them," said Morton.

AJ burst out laughing. He couldn't stop laughing and the pain in his side was something terrible, but the laughter felt so good.

Elsie came in with the tray of tea. "We'll have them for supper," she said, and took them away, leaving Morton and AJ alone.

Morton drank his tea.

"Nice flat. Homely," he said. "Reminds me of where I grew up."

"Are you here to fire me?" said AJ, battling to think of another reason for Morton's visit.

"No. I'm here to bring you three spare ribs and to tell you that Stephen has left to go to another chambers."

"Oh. Thanks," said AJ, though he couldn't for the life of him think why he was expected to care one way or the other what happened to Stephen.

"No," said Morton. "Of course I'm not here just to tell you that. I'm here to offer you a permanent job as junior clerk."

After Morton had gone, AJ sat stunned. He had been offered a job—a full-time, paid job with a future. Then why wasn't he hopping round the flat with joy? Simple. As crazy as it sounded, he was beginning to wonder which century he belonged in. He had until January to decide—perhaps time enough to find out who killed his father. And maybe find the documents that authenticated the snuffboxes. Mr. Baldwin had been sure that with them he would win the case.

AJ smiled. If he went back to the past they would be a thank-you present for Morton. If he stayed in the present they would give him a boost in his new position. And anyway, he liked the idea of Ms. Finch winning. He liked the idea a lot.

CHAPTER 27

The key.

Where was the key? The sudden realization that he no longer had it hit AJ bullet-hard. It was his only connection to his father and it was gone, his talisman lost.

Desperately he tried to retrace his steps, in his mind, at least, which wasn't easy. For the first time ever, thinking hurt his brain. He knew, logically, that he'd had it when he saw Dr. Jinx. Logically, that meant he must have had it when Moses attacked him. He felt sick. Perhaps it had fallen on the pavement. It would have been kicked aside, swept up, thrown away.

Breathe, he told himself, forgetting he had three broken ribs. Shallow breaths, then, but breathe. Think slowly. If only he could make his brain work.

The hospital had returned all his possessions to him in a plastic bag. The key wasn't in it. He searched the pockets of the clothes he had been wearing that day. Nothing. Nada. Nilch. And every other word that meant it was lost, gone, never to come back.

AJ sat on the bed and put his head in his hands. That key

gave him power that was his and his alone. Only he could lock the door and stop time leaking from one century to another. Without it, what then? He was surprised to find how unsafe the loss of the key made him feel.

Elsie found AJ on all fours, looking under his bed. She had just stuffed the turkey and was wearing an apron and yellow rubber gloves.

"What're you doing?" she asked.

"Looking for something, and it's not here," said AJ.

"Looking for what?"

"A key."

"I hung your house keys on the hook in the kitchen," said Elsie.

AJ hauled himself up into a standing position, which involved the use of his walking stick.

"No, no. Not that kind of key."

Elsie went back into the kitchen, saying she was sure it would turn up.

Oh shit. What about Slim? He couldn't remember if he'd told him about the door not being locked. What if Slim believed himself stuck in the wrong century and was desperate to come back? It would be like . . . like . . . AJ struggled for the right word through stinging-nettle fields of likes. Would Slim think to go to Ingleby's? Had he told him that was what he needed to do? It wasn't as if he could text him to explain he was in no fit state to time travel.

"Do you want a mince pie?" called Elsie from the kitchen.

AJ found himself on the brink of tears. Everything was his

fault. Slim was in the wrong century, and Leon was in deep shit over the snuffbox he'd given him. Somehow he had to sort it all out before he started work at Raymond Buildings again.

"Hark! the Herald Angels Sing" crackled out of the radio. AJ lay down, his head throbbing. He stared at a patch of mold on the wall in the corner and fell fast asleep.

Elsie had invited Jan and Roxy to join them for Christmas dinner. AJ did his best not to go into a black hole of depression over the loss of the key. His mum had made an effort, brought the wine and a Christmas pudding. Roxy came dressed in a sparkly top and skirt. Elsie had on her party frock.

"Merry Christmas," she said, opening a large bottle of Babycham and pouring glasses for Jan and AJ.

She had laid the table with paper plates and napkins and plastic wineglasses. And crackers—lots of crackers. The Christmas tree she had bought from Woolworths years ago had been taken out, dusted down and decorated with tinsel. AJ had covered it in fairy lights.

"Lovely," said Jan. "Isn't it, Roxy? Though it looks like we're having a picnic rather than Christmas dinner."

Elsie laughed. "Humbug," she said.

AJ had vivid memories of grim Christmas family fights, of Mum screaming at the top of her voice at Roxy's dad. The worst one was when Roxy's dad had pulled the tablecloth from the table just as Mum had started to carve the turkey. It was a right mess. Every year the same. Why anyone bothered, AJ had never known.

Elsie came out of the kitchen with a bird big enough to feed twenty. This was the first Christmas he could remember when there hadn't been a row before the food reached the table. Even when Roxy insisted that the TV was on while they ate and Elsie had firmly said no, to AJ's amazement Roxy didn't start whining. Elsie put her in charge of the old record player and they ate to "Ding Dong Merrily on High," not with lumps of anger in their throats but laughing and telling stories.

"Did I tell you about the time I went to Pontin's Holiday Camp?" said Elsie as she set light to the pudding.

"No," said Roxy.

"There was this fancy-dress ball and I hadn't brought anything like that with me. My Jim went as a teddy boy."

"So what did you go as?" asked Roxy.

Elsie was now slightly tipsy.

"I took the sheet of the bed and went as a nun. Nun of this, nun of that."

It was the way Elsie told them that had them all laughing. She raised her glass.

"I would like to drink a toast to absent loved ones," she said. "To my daughter, Debbie, and to my son, Norris, wherever he may be."

Jan put her hand on Elsie's arm.

"I would like to add to that. To Lucas, wherever he is."

AJ had never, ever heard his mum mention his father's name.

"My dad," he said.

"Don't sound so surprised," said Jan in her old, hard voice.

Roxy stood up.

"You forgot my dad."

But Jan couldn't quite bring herself to drink to him.

"Merry Christmas to one and all," said Elsie quickly.

After dinner, feeling more stuffed than the turkey, the four of them sat round the table pulling crackers and wearing paper hats.

"Have you heard about Leon?" said Jan.

AJ was lost in thought, wondering if it would be unwise to go to the police and ask if anyone had handed in an antique key. The mention of his friend's name brought him suddenly back into the room.

"Have you seen him?" he asked.

"No, but I hear he's in a lot of trouble," said Jan.

"He hasn't had the best of luck, that young man. And such a bright boy," said Elsie.

"There's a warrant out for his arrest."

"A warrant? How do you know?" said AJ.

"I read it in the local paper," said Jan. "Well, perhaps it's not a warrant, but the police want to question him about some stolen goods." She dropped her voice. "Between you, me and the bedpost, I heard he's upset some local gang leaders—stole their drug money."

"I don't like the sound of that," said Elsie. "I'd rather hoped he might turn up for Christmas dinner. His mum's here, waiting for him." Elsie glanced at the window. It was wet and windy outside. "Most probably Leon's with Slim."

I wish, thought AJ.

Jan and Roxy left around eight.

"That went well, don't you think?" said Elsie.

AJ helped her clean up. There wasn't much to do on account of the paper plates and plastic glasses.

Elsie sat down in the armchair with a box of chocolates and a port.

"I think," said AJ, "this has been the best Christmas ever."

They had settled down to watch TV when the flat's buzzer went.

"Who can that be?" said Elsie.

"I'll see." AJ got to his feet and limped to the intercom. "Yeah?"

"It's Leon. Let me in, man."

CHAPTER 28

Leon was soaked through and looked exhausted. The second Elsie saw him she turned on the taps in the bath.

"Get those clothes off this minute. You'll catch your death."

Leon didn't look as if he had many objections left in him.

AJ took Leon's clothes to put in the washing machine. It was as he was going through the pockets of his trousers that he found it. He sat on the kitchen floor staring at it for a long, long time. Leon had the key.

Leon came out of the bathroom wearing Elsie's candlewick dressing gown. AJ was sitting on his bed holding the key.

"It is yours, then. I thought so," said Leon. He sat down next to AJ. "I hate being dirty—it makes you feel you're part of the pavement. No name, no business, no right to be there. Only good for walking over."

"What made you pick up it up?" asked AJ.

"I saw you coming out of Dr. Jinx's. Do you know what I was about to do?"

"No," said AJ.

He wasn't sure he wanted to know.

"Kill him. And I didn't care what happened to me. I just wanted the bastard dead."

"Then why did you work for him?" asked AJ.

"'Cause I'm a jerk. I thought I could play him at his own game, give him a taste of his own medicine. Then I realized it was hopeless. He was just one little cog in a huge machine, an endless circle ruled by money. I stood no chance of breaking it. I felt so useless . . . I flipped out. I thought if I killed him at least he couldn't fuck up anyone else's life. Stupid, I know that. It wouldn't stop anything if there was no Dr. Jinx, there'd just be someone else. I bought a gun with the last of the snuffbox money. And three bullets—two for him, one for me. That's when I saw you and heard him tell you not to come back. I knew you were there looking for me, so I thought I'd follow you to explain, to tell you and Slim not to worry."

"That snuffbox," said AJ. "I'm really sorry, bro. I didn't know it would cause so much trouble."

"That snuffbox," said Leon. "Do you know how much I got for it?"

"I hope a lot," said AJ.

"More money than I ever dreamed of, and I feel real bad because I blew it. I blew the lot. I thought to myself, I'll go to Jamaica, go find my little brother. But then I'd have to get a passport, and that was tricky. Dr. Jinx was already after me when I heard that I was wanted by his boss as well. I got wasted, lost track of time, lost most of the money, bought the gun. I can't go to prison. I know that's where I'm heading. I am in so much trouble."

"Where's the gun now?" asked AJ, wondering if he had missed it when he was going through Leon's clothes. Could a gun go off on the spin cycle?

"I threw it away after what Moses and his dog did to you. I chucked it in a dog-shit bin in the park."

Leon was a handsome young man even in pink candlewick. AJ imagined him as the hero of a book or a film. He looked tortured, just like heroes do when things haven't gone right. AJ felt responsible. He had been completely naive to give Leon the snuffbox in the first place.

"If the police question you, I'll tell them I gave it to you."

"No, you must never do that. You are going to do so well in your fancy law firm, and I, as my gran would say, is destined for hell."

"I made you turkey sandwiches and a pot of tea!" shouted Elsie from the kitchen.

"Come on, it's still Christmas Day," said AJ.

Later, Elsie said goodnight and left AJ to sort out the sleeping arrangements. He took the sofa, Leon the bed.

AJ lay watching the Christmas-tree lights flash on and off. Outside, drunken people shouted at the stars. It was the first time he had allowed himself to think about Mr. Stone and the snuffbox. The lawyer hadn't been trying to fob him off. He had given him a souvenir of his dad, something precious. If only he'd known it.

He had just fallen asleep when the entryphone buzzed. It buzzed again, longer and louder. AJ woke up suddenly to find Leon, in a T-shirt and boxer shorts, looking down at him.

"It's the police, man. They've come to arrest me, I know they have."

Elsie appeared, wrapping her dressing gown round her.

"Get in the wardrobe. You can hide in there—it's got a false back. Here, I'll show you. You," Elsie said to AJ, "make sure there's not one sign of Leon anywhere, then get into bed."

By now the police were knocking on the front door. Elsie opened it. There were two police officers: a man, about six years old, as Elsie would have described him, and a woman of about five.

"If you're looking for Father Christmas, loves," she said, "he left yesterday."

"Mrs. Tapper?"

"Elsie."

"Elsie," said the policewoman, "we've had reports that a suspect might be hiding in this flat."

"What? Well, I never saw him come in." She laughed. "Get away with you. You've been at that knockoff rum down at the station."

AJ hobbled into the hall, leaning on his stick.

"What is it, Auntie Elsie?" he said.

"Nothing, love. These two young officers are looking for Marley's Ghost." Seeing the bewildered look on the officers' faces, she added, "*A Christmas Carol*. Come along, then, come in and have a poke about if you must."

AJ and Elsie stood close together, holding hands. Elsie squeezed AJ's a little tighter as the policewoman brought a chair to stand on so that she might look on the top of the wardrobe.

"Hold on a minute, Miss Marple," said Elsie. "You are taking the piss, aren't you? I was asleep in this room. Do you think someone could climb up to the second floor and in through the double-glazed windows, then hide on the top of my wardrobe without me noticing? I might not be in the first flush of youth, dear, but neither am I senile." The policewoman stepped down, embarrassed by her own eagerness. "Perhaps," said Elsie, "this suspect of yours is decked out as my Christmas tree."

When they had finished, the police officers stood in the stairwell talking, the sound of their radios bouncing off the concrete.

"Next time," said Elsie, "you'd better bring a warrant if you're going to go nosing around in my knicker drawer."

"This is for your own protection, Mrs. Tapper," said the policeman.

She waited until they had gone down the stairs before closing the front door. Leon climbed out of the wardrobe.

"That is no ordinary wardrobe, Auntie Elsie," said Leon.

"Put it like this—my Jim occasionally had his own trouble with the Old Bill. No better place to hide than at home, that's what he used to say. Cup of tea, boys?"

"I should be going," Leon said, picking up his jeans. "I can't stay here."

"Wait," said AJ.

CHAPTER 29

It was turning dark on Boxing Day when AJ caught the bus to Mount Pleasant. He'd told Leon that he had to check something out and then he would be back to take him to a place where he wouldn't be found.

"Where is this place?" asked Leon.

"I can't tell you, not yet. You have to trust me."

"How long?"

"I'll be as quick as I can," said AJ.

"Is it the same joint where Slim is hiding out?"

"Yeah."

"It must be good, then, because I went looking for Slim and I couldn't find him anywhere."

Elsie had taken more convincing. She wasn't at all keen on AJ gallivanting about town.

"You're not well enough, love. And the hospital said you needed to rest."

AJ agreed that he wasn't exactly in the peak of good health. He didn't say that his leg and ribs ached.

"I'm fine. Just fine," said AJ. "You're not to worry about me."

Then, seeing Elsie's face, added, "I'm not going to do anything stupid."

Elsie wasn't won over.

"What? You think I'm going to believe that porkie pie? You're up to something. I just hope it isn't going to get you into trouble—that wardrobe only has space for one."

AJ said, "I'm more worried about Leon and you. What if the police come back with a warrant to search the flat properly?"

"I have that covered," said Elsie. "I've invited all the busy bees and the Queen of Bodman House round for a glass of bubbly and a nut or two."

"Brazil nuts?"

"It's my dentures, love," she said. "I can't chew like I used to."

"Won't it give the game away?"

"What—about me sucking the chocolate off of nuts?"

"No, about Leon being here."

"I've seen this old world do several cycles in the washing machine of life. If people are suspicious, the best way to deal with it is to show them there's no reason to be. Leon won't mind spending a couple of hours in the back of the wardrobe."

"No," said Leon. "It'll be like being in Narnia."

Elsie chuckled.

"But without the fur coats. After that there will be no more talk about me hiding you in my flat. I'm sure of it. No more talk, no more police."

AJ tried not to think about all that could go wrong. Time wasn't on his side; neither were his ribs.

At three on the dot the busy bees turned up for a drink, a nut and a natter. AJ passed them on his way down. It had been timed that he should leave as they were arriving. They all knew he was staying there.

AJ was on a mission to find the professor. He got off the bus at the stop near the café. A sign in the window wished all its customers a happy Christmas. Through the window he could see the professor nursing a cup of tea in the neon glow. He didn't look up from the book he was reading as AJ ordered a coffee.

"Where've you been?" asked AJ. He sat down at the professor's table.

"Here and there. I was sorry to hear what happened to you. Are you recovered?"

"So-so," said AJ.

"You still have the key, then?"

AJ nodded. "I'm going back. I left my friend and . . ."

The professor wasn't listening.

"What's your game?" asked AJ. "You were the one who encouraged me to go through the door in the first place, and now you seem completely uninterested."

"Remind me, did Jack have a friend he could phone to ask what he should do when he found the giant and the hen that laid the golden eggs? No. He just had to figure it out by himself."

"That's a fairy story and this is messed-up shit. I haven't a clue who to trust." He stopped. "Sorry. That's unfair," said AJ.

The professor slowly closed his book and put it in his pocket.

"Who to trust?" said the professor, mulling over the question. "I would say Ingleby is a good man."

"How do you know?"

"He's been a loyal servant to the Jobey family."

"OK. I'm asking you what I should do, because this is beyond any reality I know."

The professor stood and put his scarf round his neck.

He took his walking stick from the back of the chair and, lifting his hat to AJ, said,

"A new face at the door, my friend,
An old key in your hand.
Will you come once more, my friend
To walk time's forbidden land?"

"What the hell does that mean?"

"A happy New Year, AJ."

AJ watched the professor disappear into the night, then finished his tea. He remembered the white feather, the sign of a guardian angel, fluttering from the professor's books that night at Gray's Inn.

I've got to trust somebody, thought AJ.

"You're the first customer I've had all day," said the woman behind the counter as AJ paid. "I tell my old man every year there's no point in opening. He says we do it in the spirit of Christmas. Personally, I think we should stay closed to the New Year."

AJ wondered if the world had lost its grip on gravity.

It was then AJ saw the huge flaw in his plan: there was no way he could climb over the fence into the car park. He was near the electronic gate when he heard whistling. A man was coming down Phoenix Place. AJ hid in the shadows as the whistling man pressed the combination on the pedestrian gate and went through to collect his car. Just before the gate eased itself shut, AJ put his walking stick in its way. He waited until he saw the car's headlights approaching and the high, skirted metal barrier rose to let the car out. The driver hadn't seen AJ; better still, he hadn't seen the stick. AJ let himself into the car park and retrieved his walking stick. As he hobbled towards the wall the fog began to rise.

CHAPTER 30

A resounding din greeted AJ as he stepped out into a different century wearing the clothes that he'd left in the cupboard under the stairs. There was no sign of Mr. Ingleby or his mother. The house was hauntingly empty.

Here it was snowing and the steps and the pavement were icy. The noise of door knockers seemed to echo round the city. Knock followed knock in rapid succession; the harsh cacophony of brass on wood sounded as if every door in London was announcing AJ's arrival. Despite his stick, he nearly lost his footing, and, his leg hurting, he walked slower than he wished towards Chancery Lane, trying to keep his balance. A gentleman coming out of his house slipped, lost his hat and almost fell. Instinctively AJ reached out for him.

"No, no," he said to AJ, brushing him off. "I have not a shilling more to give. This Boxing Day has cost me dear as it is. My knocker has been made merry use of by first the parish beadle, then the dustman, charity boys, the postman, the street sweeper, the chimney sweep, the lamplighter and finally you, a clerk. I call it daylight robbery, or begging under another name."

Of course, Boxing Day. *Sketches by Boz*. That explained the ratatat of door knockers.

"Merry Christmas," said AJ.

AJ could almost hear him say, "Humbug."

The further he walked, the more lost in his thoughts he became. Could he really live here, never to return to the electronic jungle? Maybe. If his friends did, then he would stay too. Wouldn't he?

I've one foot in the past, one foot in the future and the whole of me is stuck in the middle, undecided, he thought. Do I walk forward, do I step back?

Thick flakes of snow were falling. AJ had never seen snow cling to the streets and houses as it did here. The lamplights were so dim and some parts were not lit at all and it was hard to see where he was going. He wasn't sure if he was walking in the right direction. He supported himself on some railings. Freezing as they were, at least he felt he stood a better chance of not going over. All he needed was a broken leg to add to his injuries.

"Mr. Jobey, if I'm not mistaken. Are you taken ill, sir?"

AJ looked up. How did this stranger know who he was?

"Jeremiah Flint, at your service. You remember me? Mrs. Furby's boarder. I am sure your friend Mr. Slim will be most delighted to see you. Many a conversation we have had, wondering when you will be back from your travels."

"I'm very pleased to see you," said AJ. "More pleased than you could ever know."

"Take my arm, Mr. Jobey," said Mr. Flint. "The pavements in these snowy conditions are quite treacherous."

A smell of oranges and cloves filled the hallway of Mrs. Furby's boardinghouse. The parlor was decorated with holly and ivy, and an abundance of candles lit the charming scene before him. Mrs. Furby was playing the piano. Standing behind her, Slim was singing from a song sheet.

"The spit got up like a naked man . . ."

—This was greeted with laughter.

"And swore he'd fight with the dripping pan.
The pan got up and cocked his tail
And swore he'd send them all to jail."

"Another," cried the jolly party. "Go on, Tom—more."

All through his time in hospital, AJ's biggest worry was that he would return to find Slim totally traumatized at being abandoned there. He had imagined him gagging to get back to Stoke Newington and the twenty-first century. Yet here he was looking completely at ease. This was a Slim AJ had never seen before.

AJ's arrival in the parlor caused the party to come to a halt. Mrs. Furby gasped.

"Oh, my good lord, Mr. Jobey! What on earth has befallen you? Not highwaymen, I trust? Or worse? For you look quite done in."

Mr. Flint offered a solution.

"Nothing, I am sure, dear Mrs. Furby, that a glass of punch won't cure."

On a table stood a silver bowl, steam rising from it. Beside it was a plate of mince pies. There was a kerfuffle as chairs were moved around to make room for the new guest.

Slim said quickly, "It's all right, no need to fuss. I can see my friend needs to rest."

"Of course," said Mrs. Furby.

"I didn't mean to interrupt the celebrations," said AJ.

Everyone assured him that he had interrupted nothing, only causing them to be merrier on account of his return.

"Don't be long, Tom," said one of the guests. "We want another of your wicked songs."

AJ was hoping that his leg would be strong enough take him up the stairs to the top of the house. He longed to sit down.

"Where are you off to?" said Slim when they reached the second floor. AJ was about to heave himself up another flight. "I don't live at the top anymore. I've got a new set of rooms."

Slim showed AJ into a well-furnished chamber. It had tall, shuttered windows and wooden floorboards covered in rugs, and the two armchairs Slim had bought when he'd first arrived were arranged in front of the fire. The room was toasty warm and looked as if Slim had been living there all his life.

Mrs. Furby knocked on the door and brought in a tray with two piping-hot glasses of punch and a plate of mince pies.

"Thank you, Dora," said Slim. "Much appreciated."

Dora? AJ saw the way she smiled at Slim and thought if this wasn't the nineteenth century he would say she had the hots for him.

"If there's anything else you need, Tom, just ring the bell."

This was a whole new Slim. One AJ felt he hardly knew.

"Your name's not Tom," said AJ. "It's Toprak."

"Yeah, but I've changed it to Thomas. Thomas Slim, Esquire, a merchant. Has a good ring to it, don't you think?"

"Aren't you pissed off with me?"

"No. Should I be?" said Slim.

"Don't you want to go back?"

"Go back?" said Slim. "Why on earth would I want to go back?"

"Because of Moses," said AJ. Even as he said it he knew he wasn't making sense.

"Moses?" said Slim and laughed. "Are you bonkers? I never want to see him or his dog again."

"Moses is in prison awaiting trial. The dog's dead."

"Sweet," said Slim.

"Doesn't that make you want to return?"

Slim didn't answer. "Is the reason you're looking so peaky to do with Moses?" he asked.

"Moses beat me up and his dog thought I was Sunday dinner. I also have concussion."

"Then you should have stayed put," said Slim. "Why did you come?"

"Leon. He's in real trouble. He's wanted by Dr. Jinx and his Mr. Big Boss."

"That's heavy," said Slim. "Why didn't you bring him with you?"

"Because I wanted to check that you were all right here. Slim, sooner or later I have to lock the door and give up the key. If the door is open it messes with history and stuff like that. And anybody could get through if they found it. My grandfather and my father wanted it locked but were murdered before they could do it. It's down to me." He paused. "I owe it to my father."

"Then lock the door.

"I will when we go home."

Slim laughed. "Home? You are joking, man. Do you think I'm going back to my uncle and aunt? Never. The best thing you've ever done for me is to bring me through the door. Century reset, my life reset. I'm not going to give all this up just for a job in Dalston Market."

AJ found he was staring at his friend.

"You need to sleep, bro," said Slim kindly.

"What about Leon?" said AJ.

"Bring him here too."

"Have you been listening to me?"

"Tell me, my friend," said Slim, "what part of the return ticket do you think we're going to miss?"

CHAPTER 31

The following morning, AJ felt less achy. From his bed he could just see the snowy, smoky rooftops of London through a gap in the curtains.

Slim was already up and dressed in a new dark red coat. He looked in on AJ to say that he had to be off.

"Off where?" asked AJ.

"To work," said Slim, adjusting his muffler in the mirror.

"Work?" repeated AJ.

It hadn't occurred to him that Slim might have a job. Slim laughed at the puzzled look on AJ's face.

"What—do you think I would hang around waiting for the money to run out? No way."

"Who do you work for?"

"Mr. Jeremiah Flint. He's my boss."

"You are joking."

"Nope. He's a merchant—he recently inherited the firm when his old dad conked it. Let's put it this way: ever since, he's been running after his business without actually taking it over. Until, that is, he gave me a job. You see, bro, all those years working on my uncle's market stall have come in very handy. I've always had a nose for a deal."

"What does he sell?"

"Tea, mostly," said Slim. "But he buys too quickly, and always for too high a price. I've put an end to all that—no one is going to swindle me out of a penny. So for the first time Mr. Jeremiah Flint has some money in the bank."

AJ was amazed. Where was the Slim who couldn't wake up in the morning and dragged himself through the day like unrisen pizza dough except when he was on a skateboard? Where was the Slim of "Life is shitty, it sure ain't pretty"?

"You've changed," said AJ.

"That's stating the proverbial obvious, bro. Think about it. Back in the land of Moses and his dead dog there are two kinds of men: those who are mummy-fied and don't grow up, and those who are villainized, who grow up too soon. Here we are men. And I have the future in my pocket and tomorrow on the soles of my shoes."

"Bloody hell, Slim. You're turning into a right little philosopher."

"Leon will feel the same, you'll see. Just bring him here. And don't leave it too long."

AJ must have fallen asleep again after Slim left, for he woke to hear the church bells ringing eleven o'clock. He was determined to go back through the door while it was still light.

Downstairs, he found that Mrs. Furby had a visitor, the local beadle. His three-cornered hat sat on the table while the rest of him filled up an armchair by the fire. He reminded AJ of the Slug.

"This is Mr. Jobey," said Mrs. Furby.

The beadle halfheartedly rose from the chair and bowed.

"A pleasure, I'm sure," he said.

"Mr. Jobey, may I offer you some coffee?" said Mrs. Furby as she rang the bell for the maid.

The beadle was feasting heartily off the remains of a meat pie accompanied by a large glass of beer. When Nellie appeared he asked if it might be possible to have some of Mrs. Furby's excellent plum pudding. "It would, madam, fill the few remaining holes of hunger."

The beadle had an unattractive habit of speaking with his mouth full. "Mischief, that's what I say. Mischief has been going on in that house." He stuffed the remains of the meat pie into his mouth. "It raises questions, yes, it does indeed. As I said, mischief, mark my words."

The beadle, having eaten the pie and spoken the pie out, came to the end of his discourse. Nellie reappeared and the beadle instantly lost all interest in anything other than the plum pudding. Shortly after, he left.

AJ said his farewells to Mrs. Furby, assuring her that he would return soon. She was delighted to know she would be meeting Leon, another of Tom's dearest friends.

"Here, Mr. Jobey," she said as AJ was about to leave. "Take a newspaper to read on the stagecoach."

With much raising of hats and waving of hands, AJ set off in the direction of Clerkenwell.

At the house AJ changed his clothes, putting the ones he'd been wearing in the wicker basket under the stairs. Without much thought, he stuffed the newspaper Mrs. Furby had given him in his pocket.

———⊷———

To celebrate his return to the twenty-first century he decided to treat himself to a cup of tea and a sandwich. He walked up to the Costa at the Angel, ordered and sat down at a table. It was only then that he remembered the newspaper. He looked at it while he drank his tea and ate the sandwich. He was about to fold it away when a name in the close print caught his eye. Samuel Dalton.

He read:

> *A coroner's inquest is to be held tomorrow, 28th Decem-*
> *ber, at the Crown Tavern, Clerkenwell Green, into the*
> *death of Samuel Dalton, Esq.*
>
> *The coroner has requested the exhumation of the late*
> *Samuel Dalton's body so that it might be examined for*
> *suspected arsenic poisoning.*

The news blew Monday into the butt end of Sunday. So that's what the beadle was on about, thought AJ. The image of Mrs. Meacock came back to him with all her smarmy sweetness. In this century or any other century he could recognize a nasty piece of work, no matter how much she gilded the gingerbread.

———⊷———

Elsie's flat was empty, and for a moment AJ panicked. Perhaps the police had been round and both Elsie and Leon were down at the cop shop. He found a note attached to the fridge door by a magnet in the shape of the Sydney Opera House. It read:

Gone to get glammed up for tonight's big quiz at the Rose and Crown. Not missing that for the world or its horse. There's food in the fridge.
Elsie X

AJ had never felt as jittery as he did standing in that kitchen, every nerve end flashing, a living pinball machine. He went into Elsie's bedroom and cautiously opened the wardrobe door.

"It's me, AJ," he said to a collection of Elsie's dresses that smelled of Lily of the Valley. Leon maneuvered himself into the room, stretched and said quietly, "I'm well pleased to see you, bro."

AJ had hoped that he would be able to explain Jobey's Door to Leon in a calm, rational way. But he felt anything but calm or rational. There it went again, that pinball hitting all the bumpers, zooming into oblivion.

"I can't stay here any longer," said Leon. "You're going to have to take me now to this place where you're hiding Slim."

AJ put the kettle on.

"Not so fast. Before I do I have to explain about where I'm taking you, and it's going to sound beyond weird."

"Come on, come on, spit out," said Leon. "The police might turn up again any minute."

AJ told him the whole story, kickoff to extra time. He left nothing out. When he'd finished he expected Leon to ask questions, but he stayed silent.

"And remember, there are no bogs there, no TV, no Twitter, no PlayStation. I'm not sure if there's a white-black problem or—"

Leon stopped him. Stirring sugar into his tea, he said, "I take it there is no Dr. Jinx, and no police looking to arrest me."

"No," said AJ.

"OK. Do I strike you as someone with a lot of choices? My mum sounded more rational than you do when she was higher than a kite, but I'm desperate enough to believe you." He took a mouthful of tea. "Mum used to say that me and you and Slim had a perfume to us. She said we smelled of fatherless boys. I think she was right. My father died of booze, yours—it turns out—was murdered and Slim's—well, who the hell knows? Not Slim. AJ, I have royally messed up here. Perhaps there—wherever this 'there' is—I'd have a chance to start again."

AJ showed him the newspaper Mrs. Furby had given him. Leon read it with interest.

"This is the Dalton geezer you were just talking about?"

"Yeah. I'm out of any depth," said AJ, "and this is the place I am planning to take you to."

"So Baldwin died soon after Samuel Dalton?" said Leon.

"About nine days later."

"But he was being kept alive by modern medicine, so there is a possibility they were poisoned at the same time. You said they had dinner together at Dalton's house."

"Yes, you're right. I hadn't thought of that."

"OK," said Leon. "Let's go."

"Hold on," said AJ. "I'm not taking you to Disney World. This is a dangerous place."

"Do you know what my value is in today's society?" said Leon. "Nothing. Nada. I'm under the radar, just another loser in a hoodie, the evil of the nation. That's how I'm seen. And I don't want to be anyone's statistic. I would rather risk it in another domain. So tell me, Einstein, how do I get to this door of yours without being picked up by the feds?"

CHAPTER 32

"How about you wear something of Elsie's?" said AJ, working on Dr. Jinx's principle that if you stood out people tended not to see who you were.

"No way, man. I would look a right wanker," said Leon. "My feet are far too big."

AJ fetched the battered suitcase in which Elsie kept Jim's clothes.

"You are messing with me," said Leon.

"No, think about Dr. Jinx."

"If I think about Dr. Jinx, I think I should have killed the goddamn jackass."

"The thing is, no one will recognize you because they would never imagine seeing you dressed as a teddy boy."

The clothes that hadn't fitted AJ made Leon look like a film star.

They both burst out laughing.

AJ left a note on the fridge next to Elsie's. He didn't say anything specific about where they were going, just that he would be back in the New Year and she wasn't to worry. Leon said he'd written her a letter and pinned it to the inside of the wardrobe.

The stairwell smelled of overboiled cabbage, and music wafted from the flats, but they saw no one. It occurred to AJ that going on the bus was not the best idea. They were near the bottle banks at the gates when Leon saw two Boris bikes, abandoned and unlocked.

"You up for this?" he asked.

"Is there a choice?"

Avoiding all the main roads, they cycled through the back streets of Islington and down to Exmouth Market. The car park had emptied out by the time they reached it, and AJ's leg and ribs were hurting worse than ever. He looked at the fence with a sinking heart.

"I don't know how I'm going to do this."

Leon considered the problem. There was no other way to get in.

"You have to," he said. "Otherwise . . ."

"There is no otherwise," said AJ.

Leon helped him up onto his shoulders and with one mighty and painful effort AJ heaved himself over the fence, trying not to scream in agony as he landed, breathless, on the other side.

"What now?" said Leon, brushing down Jim Tapper's best suit as he joined AJ.

AJ hobbled over to the wall with the lintel. Nothing happened. They stood for an age in the orange darkness as a soft, drizzly rain began to fall. Perhaps, he thought, this time there would be no fog, no door, and they would be stuck in this car park, sitting ducks for the lens of the CCTV camera. It would only take someone to report them and it would all be over for Leon.

Leon didn't say a word.

Slowly it began. So slowly that at first neither of them was aware of the fog. Then it was there. Jobey's Door. The stone face stared down at them.

Inside, the hall was gloomy. They heard voices from the room on the first floor. Leon froze. He hadn't spoken since the fog descended.

AJ called, "Mr. Ingleby? Mr. Ingleby, is that you?"

A candle flickered, light reluctantly spilt down the stairs and a cat padded slowly towards them, rubbing its back against the banisters. Ingleby's mother appeared.

"Mr. Jobey." Her voice was firmer than before. "Your friend cannot go about town dressed like that. It would never do." The cat curled round her skirts. "Would it, my beloved?" she cooed at it.

"Where is Mr. Ingleby?" asked AJ.

"Where nearly all of London has gone to stretch its ears and find out if Mr. Dalton was poisoned. He's attending the inquest at the Crown Tavern." She picked up the cat. "You have a visitor, anxious to talk to you."

"Me?" said AJ.

"Well, it isn't the Queen of Sheba he wants to speak with."

AJ climbed slowly up the rickety staircase.

"You know," said Leon who was behind him, "I don't think this property is all that sound."

"Just remember it's my house you're slagging off," said AJ.

In Ingleby's chamber a man was standing with his back to them, warming his hands at the fire.

Nonsuch spun round. He stared at Leon.

"I'm half Jamaican," Leon said defensively. "Do you have a problem, mate?"

"No," said Nonsuch. "It's just . . ."

"Annie Sorrell was Esme Dalton's mother, wasn't she?" asked AJ quickly.

"Yes. Who told you?"

"You. You just confirmed what I suspected," said AJ.

"You're a smart one." Nonsuch sat down, defeated. "What the hell. I've made a right mess of things." With a ball and chain of a sigh he began. "Yes, Annie was Esme's mother. When I saw her brought to the gallows, I lost it. I tried to stop the hanging, attacked some officials, wanted to fight the world for what they were going to do to my Annie. After that I remember nothing until I woke up in prison. I was sentenced to deportation for seven years, and I swore that once I'd done my time I would come back and find my little girl, tell her that her mother was innocent. Annie couldn't have killed the Jobey family."

"How do you know?"

"Annie couldn't read or write—she was bright but uneducated. She knew nothing about poisons, and whoever killed the Jobeys did. Lucas was my best friend. If for one moment I believed Annie was guilty then I would have said justice had been done that day, regardless of my love for her. She never did it. There were footprints in that room that didn't belong to the family, but no one was interested, and for all Ingleby's efforts and Mr. Stone's, she went to the gallows. She was buried in Newgate Prison and I was sent to Australia."

"How did you get back?" asked AJ.

"I did my time and then worked hard to earn the money for my passage home. When we docked I was broke and needed to make some dough. I fell in with a bad crowd, did a few things I'm not proud of, and now I'm a wanted man. I had no one to turn to except Ingleby. All I want to do is to take my daughter home."

His gaze fixed on Leon again.

"Where is home?" asked Leon.

And then it struck AJ that it wasn't Leon Nonsuch was staring at but the clothes he was wearing. Jim Tapper's jacket was a tad on the bright side—chemical blue with black velvet pockets and collar. AJ could see it might appear weird in any age—but the spinners in the pinball machine of AJ's mind began to light up, to make connections.

It was obvious. How could he have been so thick? The twinkle in Nonsuch's eyes might have been extinguished, but nevertheless they were Elsie's eyes.

"I would guess home is the twenty-first century," said AJ. "And you're on the wrong side of the door."

CHAPTER 33

Nonsuch wiped the back of his hand across his eyes.

"Those clothes—they belonged to my dad. Mum kept them in a suitcase on top of her wardrobe."

"You're Norris Tapper," said Leon.

"My mum . . . I can't bring myself to ask . . . is she . . ."

"Auntie Elsie, as we call her," said Leon, "is all dolled up and sitting in the Rose and Crown doing the Christmas Quiz."

"Trust my old mum to be still going strong," said Norris, sniffing. "And Debbie?"

"Coincidentally," said AJ, "she buggered off to Australia. She's not great at keeping in touch. But she sent Elsie a Sydney Opera House fridge magnet for Christmas."

"Nothing changes," said Norris, a flicker of a long-extinguished smile crossing his face.

Downstairs the front door closed. Norris jumped.

"It's me!" shouted Ingleby, his step on the stairs rattling the walls.

He appeared in the chamber, out of breath, followed by His Honor.

"You must leave now," Ingleby said to Norris. "That rat of a man at the Red Lion—I knew he was not to be trusted. The police raided the Red Lion this morning, searching for you."

"You mean the man we met at the inn near the Fleet?" asked AJ.

"The very same, and if I see him again he will be joining the shit at the bottom of the Fleet. The reward on Nonsuch's head was too tempting for vermin like that." Ingleby noticed Leon. "The last of your friends, I hope, Mr. Jobey?"

"Yes. Mr. Ingleby, this is Leon."

"A pleasure," said Ingleby. "Excuse my manners, but we have a pressing problem on our hands, and if some solution isn't found Nonsuch here will be arrested."

"What does it matter now?" said Norris. "It's all over."

"It matters a lot to your mum," said AJ. "She's never given up hope. She's kept your bedroom just as it was, believing one day you'd come home. I don't want to have to tell her that I saw you hang at Newgate."

"So you've told them?" said Ingleby.

"I want to see Esme, just once," said Norris.

"The beadle is snooping about," said Ingleby. "That means the police won't be far behind."

It was Leon who took charge of the situation. To AJ's astonishment, he stripped off to his boxers.

"Give me your clothes," he said to Norris, "and put your dad's on."

"I won't go without seeing her."

"You have no choice," said Ingleby. The room, the house and all began to echo to the sound of someone banging at the back door.

Reluctantly Norris did as he was told.

They could hear Ingleby's mother in the hallway.

"What is all the fuss about? Is London on fire?"

"Come on, mate," said Leon. "And watch out for the CCTV cameras."

He and AJ took one of Norris's arms each and bundled him downstairs.

AJ opened the door and for a moment caught a glimpse of the twenty-first century as Norris Tapper stepped out into his future.

CHAPTER 34

The beadle, all puffed up, a stuffed turkey of pompous authority, warmed himself by the fire.

"There has been a report," he said to Ingleby, "that a certain
wanted man is hiding in these premises." He looked at AJ and
then at Leon. Norris's worn clothes did him no favors.

"My name is Jobey, sir. We met at Mrs. Furby's over a plum
pudding," said AJ.

The beadle, a man whose stomach had more intellect than
his brain, sighed.

"An exceedingly good plum pudding. One of the finest I
have had the pleasure of tasting." He turned to Leon. "Who
might this be?"

"This is Mr. Leon Grant," said AJ. "A highly educated young
man who has been traveling. He has just arrived in London."

"Indeed," said the beadle. "That would, I suppose, explain
the condition of your attire."

"Yes," said Leon. He said it as if it was final, no more questions
necessary.

The beadle, unsatisfied with the lean answer he had been
given, was working up to fattening it with more questions when

Ingleby's mother appeared, surrounded by cats and bringing with her the pungent smell of cats' piss.

"Mother," said Ingleby angrily. "What have I said about your felines and their proximity to His Honor?"

The magpie spread its wings in agreement.

The beadle sneezed.

"I cannot . . . ," he said and sneezed again. "Cats," he managed to say, despite watery eyes and a runny nose. Then, giving up all notions of searching the premises, said he must be gone.

Leon waited until Ingleby and the beadle had left the room and Ingleby's mother had disappeared down the back staircase.

"This is awesome," he said.

"Yes, but there's no bog, no Internet, no mobile," AJ reminded him. "And no skateboards."

"Your point?" said Leon.

"You won't like it here. There's terrible poverty. And slavery."

"What? And you think there isn't where we've just come from? It's the same, bro, only hidden by better drains and deodorants. But underneath there's not much difference. And I have an advantage—I have seen the future."

Ingleby was in the doorway, listening.

"I agree," he said. "I would not live in your world, Mr. Jobey. It smells of something far worse than unwashed bodies; it stinks of loneliness." He went to a cabinet and poured them each a glass of wine. "Welcome to 1830, Leon Grant, Esquire. Mother," he called. "We cannot have Mr. Grant dressed like this."

"I know, I know," she said coming back upstairs, without the cats.

AJ had believed that mother and son couldn't stand one another. It was only now that he saw how wrong he was.

"I've brought His Honor his dinner. The beadle left."

"Yes, Mother dear. How clever of you to remember his dislike of cats. The minute he sniffed them he was gone. But we have a small problem that could trip us up and send us flying. The solution comes in the shape of a suit of clothes for this young man."

Mrs. Ingleby sized up Leon.

"You had better come with me," she said to him.

When Leon reappeared, the transformation was surprising. He was the most handsome dandy in London town.

Mrs. Ingleby giggled. "The young man was made for this century. Sir, you will have half the ladies in the metropolis swooning at your feet."

"Mother, please," said Ingleby.

Leon was grinning as if Arsenal had just won the FA Cup.

CHAPTER 35

The Iron Duke himself might have arrived at Mrs. Furby's for all the fuss that was made of Leon. It was hard for AJ and Slim to keep a straight face, especially when Ingleby solemnly announced that they where honored to have such a well-educated gentleman come to stay.

Mrs. Furby, holding on to the back of an upright chair, said, "My word—and a friend of yours, Tom?"

There followed a prologue of apologies about the humbleness of her boardinghouse and its virtue lying in its being clean.

"Humble but clean," Mrs. Furby kept repeating, still gripping the chair for support.

AJ supposed she was in fear of being overcome completely by the presence of such a fine young man.

Even Mrs. Downie and her daughter Flora, who both found putting more than one word in front of another somewhat tricky, suddenly discovered their fledgling voices and started chirping together, wondering if the gentleman shouldn't be given their rooms. They were more than happy to move upstairs. Leon listened to all this nonsense, unable to believe it. Seeing that it wasn't going to stop anywhere short of New Year, he made an attempt to pop all their balloons of high expectations.

"Mrs. Furby," he said flatly. "I have returned from a long and difficult journey and—"

"Highwaymen?" she interrupted.

Leon shook his head. "I have been abroad," he said.

"Oh—you have been overseas," said Mrs. Furby with relief.

Slim warmed to the idea that Leon had returned from a voyage to distant lands.

"Yes," he said, "and my friend lost everything when his ship was sunk by pirates. All his belongings and, worse still, his mother, who he did his best to save."

A glare from Leon stopped Slim from further flights of fancy, but to Mrs. Furby and the boarders Leon appeared as the best kind of hero, one who had tried and failed.

Slim began to regret advertising Leon's bravery. Dora appeared quite overcome by all that had befallen him.

"That is truly terrible," she said as she rang the bell for refreshments.

Nellie entered with the tea tray and promptly turned bright red when she saw Leon. She even made a little curtsy as she put the tray on a side table.

Slim, whose nose was definitely out of joint, touched the teapot and said, "Did you boil the water?"

"As good as near, sir," said the maid.

"It has to boil. How many times must I tell you? And did you filter the water?"

"I forgot, sir, in the excitement."

Slim handed the tray back to the maid. She looked at Mrs. Furby.

"Nellie," said Mrs. Furby firmly. "You will do as Mr. Slim asks. The water must be filtered, then boiled for two minutes or longer. Preferably longer."

"Sorry, ma'am," said Nellie.

"Let us have wine instead. A celebration," suggested Mrs. Furby.

As Nellie went to fetch wine and glasses, Mr. Flint explained Tom's extraordinary system of filtering water.

"You saw the bottom off a glass bottle, then stuff the neck with cotton rag and add charcoal. I tell you, it's a miracle. Even the brown water from the River Fleet becomes as clear as glass. A magician couldn't perform a better trick." He clapped his hands together and lowered his voice. "I am thinking of finding a way to market it. Since we have been using Tom's 'water purifying method,' as he calls it, not one of us has been ill—quite a feat in this metropolis."

Mrs. Downie, having taken one glass of wine, found her tongue to be positively sailing away with her.

"It's a terrible business, would you not agree, Mr. Flint? Cholera has reached St. Petersburg. I am frightened that it will not be long before London succumbs to this terrible disease and that we will all be brought to our deaths by it."

"Not if you purify the water and boil it," said Slim.

"Mr. Slim, that is not what I have heard. You catch it through a miasma."

"A smell?" said Leon, and burst out laughing. "You are joking!"

"It is no laughing matter," said Mrs. Downie.

She brought out a handkerchief and dabbed at invisible tears.

"There, there," said Mr. Flint kindly.

"Keep drinking Mr. Flint's teas," Slim added, "and you'll stay in the rudest of health."

Flora was thrilled by the turn in the conversation. All things morbid interested her greatly.

"I have heard a rumor that the daughter of a Mr. Dalton of St. John Street is quite mad and poisoned her father."

"Flora," said Mrs. Downie, "that is nothing more than gossip."

"No it's not," said Flora, bringing out a cheap pamphlet.

This was Flora's moment in the spotlight. She read out loud: "'To think of the awful suffering of the housekeeper, living in fear that she will be the next to be given arsenic.'"

"That is just the kind of nonsense that appears in those publications," said Ingleby.

"'Dr. Seagrave,'" continued Flora, "'is to go to the house in St. John Street tomorrow to have Miss Dalton committed to an asylum.'"

"Rubbish!" said Ingleby. "There was no mention of that today at the inquest."

This is all to do with that bloody will, thought AJ.

Flora was annoyed at not being taken seriously and changed the subject.

"Do you believe in ghosts?" Flora asked Leon.

"No. Vampires, maybe."

"Vampires! Oh—how wonderful."

AJ bowed out of the conversation. Tomorrow he would go to the Dalton house and try to see Miss Esme. If there was any truth in the rumors then she needed help.

By the time they had said their goodnights it was past midnight. Leon stared round at Slim's chamber.

"All this is yours, plus two bedrooms and a bog?"

"Water closet," replied Slim. "It's a bit primitive, but I'm working on it."

Leon collapsed in an armchair.

"This," he said, "is well rad. But I haven't a penny to my name, so how am I going to live here?"

"Remember Dick Whittington?" said Slim.

"What planet are you on?"

"That cat of his was one clever dude. He made everybody believe his master was the Marquis of Carabas."

"Dick Whittington was the mayor of London, and Puss in Boots is a fairy story," said Leon.

"And this isn't?" said Slim.

Leon laughed. AJ realized that he hadn't heard him laugh for a very long time.

"You're right," said Leon. "I like your bird—she's one hell of an improvement on Sicknote."

"I don't have a bird," said Slim, going red. "If you mean Dora, she's not my girl. She's a widow. Anyway, she wouldn't want me."

"Wrong. She does," said Leon. "I tell you, bro, one day she will be all yours."

Slim grew a little in height.

"You think so?"

"I know so."

AJ wished that he could relax and enjoy the three of them being together again, but he couldn't.

"You know," said Leon, "this pacing back and forth is giving me carpet sickness. Could you stop? Is it about that girl Esme Dalton?"

AJ nodded.

"She was definitely not mad when I last saw her," he said. "The housekeeper, Mrs. Meacock, on the other hand, gave me the creeps. If I heard she'd lost her marbles I wouldn't find it at all surprising."

"Madness interests me," said Leon. "I read Freud and Jung trying to find out why Mum was an addict. I thought they might know how to sort her out."

"You're into psychiatry?" said Slim.

"Yeah. There was no one else to help with Mum except Freud. He'd treated addictive personalities like hers. Perhaps now that she's dead she's lying on his couch taking in the wisdom that sure was lacking in her life."

CHAPTER 36

The following morning Slim had gone to work and Leon was still fast asleep when AJ left Mrs. Furby's.

Outside it was snowing and two little boys were throwing snowballs. A snowball hit AJ's coat, and laughing, the boys ran away. In the confusion of vehicles the snow was turning to watery slush. AJ hailed a hackney cab and with some difficulty pulled himself up and into the seat.

"St. John Street," he said, hoping that he wasn't too late and that Miss Esme hadn't already been taken away.

It would help, he thought, if the mobile phone had been invented. A calling card didn't quite do it. The hackney cab pulled up outside the Daltons' house and AJ had the presence of mind to ask the driver to wait, saying he would treble the fare.

He rang the doorbell. It was opened by Miss Esme's maid, Agnes. It was obvious she had been crying.

"Is Miss Esme at home?" AJ said.

"No," said the maid, sniffing. "No one is at home to visitors."

AJ's heart sank. "Do you mean she is at home and not seeing anyone, or she is not actually on the premises? I need to know—it's urgent."

The maid stifled a sob.

"Please would you tell her it's Aiden Jobey?"

The door was closed.

How do you ever see anyone in this city? thought AJ irritably. Or, more to the point, see them alone?

He was waiting, not sure what to do, when the door opened again and the maid, her head darting this way and that, said, "Quickly, sir, come in."

AJ didn't wait to be told where to go. He went straight up the stairs. Miss Esme was on the landing to meet him.

"Was it you?"

"Was it me what?"

"Was it you who told the beadle that you suspected my father was poisoned?"

"No, of course not. Why would I? You said the doctor had diagnosed an infection."

Miss Esme sighed.

"It was her, then." To the maid she said, "Keep a lookout for Mrs. Meacock."

"I've packed a bag for you, Miss Esme. Come now, she'll be back soon," said Agnes.

"What happened?" AJ asked as he followed Miss Esme into the drawing room.

"Someone told the beadle that they were certain that my father was poisoned, and the coroner requested that my father's body be exhumed. The inquest will be reconvened today. Mrs. Meacock has taken the carriage to fetch Dr. Seagrave. She will have him sign the papers to say I am insane."

"Please, Miss Esme, we must go," called Agnes.

"I agree," said AJ. Miss Esme looked so vulnerable. "Let's get the hell out of here."

"What does that mean?" asked Miss Esme.

"It means you and me leave before Mrs. Meacock comes back with the doctor and they have you locked up."

"That would be as good as confessing to murder."

"No, it would just give us time to find out the truth."

"Miss Esme," called Agnes. "Be quick, the carriage is coming down the street."

"There isn't time to argue about it," said AJ.

"No," said Miss Esme. "I am innocent, and I refuse to be blamed for something I didn't do."

AJ heard Mrs. Meacock's voice in the hall.

"And we will prove it," he said, "but right now—"

The drawing-room door opened and Mrs. Meacock came in, accompanied by a small man wearing a full wig.

"Mr. Jobey," said Mrs. Meacock. "I am so sorry that you find us in this state. I must ask you to leave right away."

"Mr. Jobey is my guest," said Miss Esme, her voice shaking. "And this is my house."

"Was, my dear," said Mrs. Meacock, "until you went mad and murdered your father. Better by far that you go with Dr. Seagrave than go to the gallows."

"I am not mad. I never have been mad," said Miss Esme.

AJ took hold of her hand.

"We're going," he said.

The unexpected nature of his sudden decision took everyone by surprise. It wasn't hard to push past Mrs. Meacock or the doctor, who was too taken aback to resist. AJ slammed the drawing-room door and locked it. As he and Miss Esme ran down to the hall, they saw three burly men waiting by the open door. Beyond them in the street stood AJ's hackney cab.

AJ wasn't up for a fight. He took a handful of coins from his pocket.

"How much to scram?" he asked.

Two men took what was offered. That left only the third, who was made of gristle and muscle and looked as if he beat up bears for a living. He had a leather strap in his hand, but before he was close enough to do any damage with it he was soaked by the contents of a chamber pot thrown from the landing by Agnes.

The hackney cab driver helped Miss Esme into the cab and AJ struggled in after her.

"Where to?" asked the driver.

At that moment, they heard a cry.

"Miss Esme! Miss Esme, please don't leave me here."

AJ opened the door again and pulled in Agnes and her box.

"Mount Pleasant," he said to the driver. "As fast as you can."

As the hackney cab sped away, AJ looked back to see Mrs. Meacock gesticulating from the drawing-room window. Her words were lost to him.

CHAPTER 37

AJ could only imagine that Ingleby must have known they were coming, for the hall, usually devoid of heat or light, had both. In the grate a fire had been lit, as had the broken chandelier. The light did little more than confirm AJ's fears that the whole building was on the verge of toppling down. He could imagine the house featured in one of those upmarket magazines for people who had enough money to indulge in dreams, but he realized Miss Esme and Agnes would find the idea of decay being fashionable tricky to understand.

They stood, a small, shipwrecked party washed into a crumbling hall.

"Where are we?" Agnes asked.

"Mr. Ingleby's house," said AJ.

Right on cue, Mr. Ingleby rushed up the back stairs.

"Welcome," he said breathlessly, but with such heartfelt meaning that there was no more to be said about the dust and decrepitude of the building. He led them up to a drawing room that AJ had not seen before. It was full of furniture, all of which looked out of place and added to the general awkwardness felt by everyone there.

Even His Honor looked as if he had been spruced up for the occasion of Miss Esme's visit.

Ingleby started to explain that he himself had planned to bring Miss Esme to safety and to that end he had hired the third thug to stop anyone who tried to snatch her.

"Oh, my," said Agnes. "I emptied a chamber pot over him."

"Yes," said Ingleby. "And I had to pay him double."

All of them laughed and the awkwardness started to dispel.

Mrs. Ingleby arrived with a tray of glasses and a bottle of her best elderflower wine. She seemed to be completely attired in someone else's clothes that neither fitted nor suited her, and the whole ensemble was pulled together by another melodrama of a hat. So striking was her appearance that Agnes was unable to help herself, and let out a gasp. Her reaction upset neither mother nor son but rather confirmed to Mrs. Ingleby what she had first suspected on seeing Miss Esme, that none of her rooms were suitable for such ladylike company.

AJ saw Miss Esme looking nervously at the magpie, flinching when it stretched its wings.

Ingleby saw it too and said, "His Honor won't hurt you, Miss Esme."

"Forgive me," she said, "but my mother was frightened of birds, especially magpies. She thought one was haunting her. When they came to take her to the asylum, she screamed that it was the bird that had stolen her reason."

AJ moved nearer to Miss Esme, then held out his hand, not knowing if His Honor would leave Ingleby's shoulder. To his surprise the magpie flew and rested on AJ's outstretched arm. Some moments, AJ reckoned, stood outside the logic of time and space, too important to belong to the dullness of minutes and seconds. With His Honor on his arm and Miss Esme's hand—tentatively at first—stroking the bird's head, this was such a moment. Her gray eyes met his and he felt a tug on his heart.

Then it was over. Time rewound itself and the magic of that moment was gone. Had she felt it too? She must have done.

"I'll leave you to settle in," said AJ. "And call on you tomorrow if that's all right."

AJ bowed as he left the room, and thought as he made his way down the stairs that he was beginning to get into the swing of things. Ingleby followed him, His Honor perched once more on his shoulder.

"Your father would have been very proud of you today, Mr. Jobey, as am I," he said.

"Thanks," said AJ, trying to sound casual, which was hard, as he rarely received compliments. He wrapped his muffler round his neck. "There's something I want to ask you."

"What, Mr. Jobey?"

"I've been wondering . . . was it His Honor Annie Sorrell saw that day at my grandfather's house?"

"I couldn't say. He wasn't my bird then. But he had belonged to someone, that is certain, for he was very tame. I came across His Honor—near Smithfield it was—about ten years ago. He was as near dead as a creature could be, weren't you, my poor *Pica pica*?"

The magpie let out a cry.

"I revived him and he took it into that clever head of his that I was his savior and decided to take a peck at life again."

AJ headed back to Mrs. Furby's. If only his bones would stop hurting he might be able to think straight.

Should he tell Miss Esme that there was a door that led to the future, to a place where her real father and her grandmother lived, where she would be loved? The past is all there, he thought, at the touch of a search button, whereas the future takes some explaining. Most probably she would cling to the furniture, refuse to budge and take her chances of proving her sanity to the doctors rather than with some nutter who claimed he could travel through time. Perhaps he should instead concentrate on how to tell her about her real parents.

His muffler, his supposed protector against the snowy rain, had failed in its duty, and he felt the damp seeping through. His arm and leg ached something rotten. His coat was water-logged and heavy, and he found himself limping, wishing he'd brought the stick. There was no escaping it—he couldn't miss his hospital appointment. If there had been time he would have had his dressings changed before he brought Leon through Jobey's door.

Here you are in London in 1830, he thought, with a young woman in real trouble, worrying about a hospital appointment in the twenty-first century. It's bonkers.

Other people went abroad, took package holidays, had road trips and saw America. He had been nowhere, except once to Blackpool, and that was a shock. He had imagined the sea would be blue; it was gray. It had rained, and Roxy's dad was arrested for being drunk and disorderly. Happy family memories. He was doing something more extraordinary than anyone with a first-class ticket had ever achieved: he had traveled in time, walked painlessly through two centuries and back again. It wasn't a journey he could tell many people about without being seen as one of the loony tunes in Clissold Park. The camera hadn't been invented; any souvenir would look like he'd got it in an antiques shop. If he sent a postcard it would never arrive.

To him this London felt like a foreign land: intriguing but with a language and manners that baffled him. He was genuinely surprised that Slim had taken to this nonelectronic jungle with such ease, as if all along he was meant to be in this century. Why was it, then, that he, AJ, felt uneasy here? Perhaps he needed to get to know the place better. After all, it was his inheritance, his door, his key. Perhaps all travel was like this—disjointed, as if fragments of you had been scattered across time.

The day was running out of light, and AJ watched a theater of windows reveal different scenes. A family sat down to eat in a cozy glow. In a basement he could make out the hands of a cook as she stuffed a chicken. In another window a man took a book from a shelf, and in another two cats were preening themselves. All of this life went on, went backwards, went forwards, a seesaw of time.

He was near Chancery Lane when he felt a hand on his shoulder. He spun round.

"Slim," he said. "What's happening, man?"

"Nothing special. I'm just on my way home from work."

"You really like it here, don't you? Don't you miss your city, your skateboard, your family?" asked AJ.

"You know, I've sort of forgotten about it all."

"You can't have. It hasn't been that long."

"Tell me, what is there to be all mixed-up nostalgic about? I can't remember a time, even as a kid, when I opened the front door to find someone who wanted to see me. Or to find anyone there at all."

"It's a major step," said AJ.

"It's just like emigrating to America."

"Come on, Slim—really?"

"One day while you were gone I took Dora in a hackney carriage to Stoke Newington. Do you know, it's a village with farms, fields and a huge common. Children were playing in the snow and it looked like one of those glittery Christmas cards that Auntie Elsie has on her mantelpiece. Except I was in it. And I thought, yes, this is where I want to live, in this here and now. I tell you, the only thing I will miss is you, bro, nothing else. It's that simple." He opened Mrs. Furby's front door and they were greeted by the smell of cinnamon and honey. "Come on, let's get warm."

CHAPTER 38

"Oh, Tom, there you are. I've been waiting for you," said Mrs. Furby, coming out of the parlor. "Waiting for you both," she added.

"Is Leon here?" asked AJ.

"No, he went out for a walk. A quiet one, is Mr. Grant. I think he is still grieving for his mother. Now take off your wet clothes and come and sit by the fire. You look half frozen, Mr. Jobey, and too pale, if you don't mind me saying."

The parlour was snug and the lamplight flattered the room, softening the corners. Sitting near the fire was a woman much older than Mrs. Furby, who AJ recognized as the nurse he'd seen that first morning at Samuel Dalton's house.

"This," said Mrs. Furby, "is my dear friend Mrs. Renwick."

Mrs. Renwick's starched bonnet was doing its level best to define some features of note in her kindly pudding of a face, but it was her hands that interested AJ, for they were red raw with scrubbing.

"These are the two gentlemen I told you about," said Mrs. Furby. "Mr. Slim and Mr. Jobey."

"Jobey?" said Mrs. Renwick, not moving from her cozy seat. "A pleasure, I am sure."

"Mrs. Renwick is a nurse," explained Mrs. Furby. "She boarded here for two years."

"The nicest lodgings I have had in the whole of London," said Mrs. Renwick. She had a ponderous way of talking, as if each word mattered and needed time to be heard before bothering to join it up with the next.

"Sit, gentlemen, sit," said Mrs. Furby. "I will ring for tea."

Nellie looked as pleased as punch when she brought in the tray.

"I filtered the water twice, Mr. Slim, and boiled it for five minutes precisely," she said.

"Perfect," said Mrs. Furby. She poured the tea and, handing the nurse a cup, said, "Would you mind telling Mr. Jobey and Mr. Slim the story you have just told me?"

"I see no point in repeating the sorry tale. It won't make it any better and could make it worse by hearing it all again."

"Mr. Jobey, I know, would be interested to hear it. He is acquainted with Miss Dalton."

"The words of the dying are not to be trusted," said Mrs. Renwick. She stood up. "I should be going. I just brought Dora some Madeira wine sent me by a well-wisher and, as Dora knows, I do not drink."

"Please," said AJ, "I want to hear what happened. I saw you when I came with another gentleman, Mr. Ingleby, to visit Mr. Dalton."

"So you did, sir. I thought I recognized you." Mrs. Renwick

sat down again and began with a loud sigh. "There wasn't half a rumpus after you left. Mrs. Meacock had Miss Esme locked in her room, and then she said to me that on no account was Mr. Dalton to have any more visitors. She stood at the end of his bed with this smile on her face and said, 'You've brought this on yourself, Samuel.' And with that she was gone. Two days I looked after him. It was a slow and painful death. He asked me, over and over again, if Mrs. Meacock was in the house. When I said she was, poor Mr. Dalton became most agitated and whispered, 'Don't let her near me.'

"I have looked after those coming into the world and those leaving. Often you find those that are sick with fever speak with tongues that belong half to this world and half to Hades, for all the sense they make. Once he asked me if I could see Mrs. Meacock in the room. I told him there was no one there and he begged me to look outside the door, for he was sure he heard rustling. What I heard outside was laughter that came from the dining room. I saw trays of food were being taken to Mrs. Meacock and Dr. Seagrave."

Leon had come in quietly and stood leaning against the mantelpiece.

"I am not a woman of imagination. I have no story to tell, none worth listening to. Neither do I believe in ghosts, but even without the extravagance of imagination, I have never seen a man more terrified of anyone than Mr. Dalton was of Mrs. Meacock. Two hours before he died he started talking to someone who he called . . ." The nurse paused and looked at AJ. ". . . Old Jobey."

"As I said, I'm not a woman of imagination, and it bothers

me little as to who the dying wish to converse with. Mr. Dalton said, 'I did not do it, Old Jobey. I would not have done that to you. I swear I didn't know . . . I didn't know until they had hanged her.' His last words before he died were 'The will . . . it was the will.'

"I went to tell Mrs. Meacock that her master was dead and I found her and Dr. Seagrave were . . . well, I will say nothing other than drunk. I was disgusted. I laid out Mr. Dalton and left."

"May I ask a question?" said Leon.

The nurse nodded.

"In your professional opinion, was Mr. Dalton poisoned?"

"I couldn't say for sure, sir. But if he was, I know who poisoned him, and it wasn't that young girl."

CHAPTER 39

The following morning, after one of Mrs. Furby's excellent breakfasts, Leon sat in a chair in Slim's rooms, his long legs stretched out before him.

"I've been thinking," he said. "I remember reading about a woman murderer. She poisoned three of her four husbands."

"Blimey," said Slim. "Did no one click what she was up to?"

"Eventually. Only when they found her notebooks. She'd kept records of how long it took each of her husbands to die. She took out life insurance on each one, and when another one hit the dust she claimed her money, steadily becoming richer with each passing husband. Motive, that's what you need."

"Like Dalton's will," said AJ.

"We should start by seeing Miss Esme."

"I have to go to work," said Slim. "But is there anything I can do from there?"

"You can see if any of the many grocery shops that Mr. Flint supplies has sold arsenic to the Dalton household," said Leon.

The three newly minted gents were about to set off when Mrs. Furby opened the parlor door to inquire if they would be back for dinner.

"I'm not sure," said AJ. "I hope so."

He noticed that the wine Mrs. Renwick had brought Mrs. Furby sat unopened on a side table. Somewhere deep in his subconscious an alarm bell rang, but he forgot about it in the effort to hail a cab.

This was the winter of 1830, and AJ remembered that it was on this time that Charles Dickens would base Christmas at Dingley Dell in *The Pickwick Papers*. It was one of the frostiest winters on record, and that morning London lay muffled under a thick eiderdown of snow and ice.

"I don't think that I'll ever get my head round how amazing this is," said Leon as they clip-clopped slowly towards Ingleby's house. "It feels like I'm floating in another world, that I've been given a clean sheet of paper to write a new future on."

"Don't worry," said AJ. "The gravity of the situation will strike you soon enough."

Clip-clop, clip-clop. London was bathed in that pale wintry sunlight that can only belong to a snowy December. They stared out the windows, Leon mesmerized by all he saw. Several carriages had skidded and ended up facing the wrong way, their bewildered horses waiting to be untangled, steam pouring from their nostrils.

Finally they arrived at Mr. Ingleby's. Leon waited in the hall, as AJ was keen to see Miss Esme alone and try to explain about her father and mother.

Upstairs in the drawing room, surrounded by cats, Mrs. Ingleby sat in the wintry light, which showed every line, crevice and wrinkle on her well-aged face. Miss Esme sat opposite her in a wingback chair, reading a book, and, in that instant before she realized that AJ was there, he had a revelation. The same light that did Mrs. Ingleby no favors showed Miss Esme's face to perfection. He felt once again that tug, stronger than before, something shifting in the tectonic plates of his heart. This had never happened with Alice Fisher.

AJ had gone out with her for a whole year and never once in all those twelve dull months had he felt a pull, let alone a tug, of anything other than guilt. She was so clingy that Leon had nicknamed her Ivy. AJ would ask her what she wanted to do, and her reply was always the same: "I don't mind. Whatever you want to do."

Round and round the mulberry bush they would go, until finally AJ could stand it no more and told her he wanted to be on his own. After that, he reckoned girlfriends were overrated, a waste of space compared to his two best friends, but this morning—either due to the watery sunlight or the tug—he felt somehow different. He knew that if he ever asked Miss Esme what she wanted to do she would tell him.

She looked up from the book and said, "Mr. Jobey. I am pleased to see you. Agnes has something I want to show you. I'll go and fetch it."

Mrs. Ingleby rose, saying she would ask Agnes and it was no trouble at all, in fact her legs needed stretching. She left the room followed by an entourage of cats.

AJ, finding himself tongue-tied, stumbled badly and instead of his well-rehearsed speech, said, "You don't belong here." To which Miss Esme looked completely bemused. AJ was just warming up to telling her who her real parents were, when Agnes came in with Leon and Mr. Ingleby, His Honor perched like a macabre hat upon his head.

"Here it is, Miss Esme," said Agnes, looking decidedly sheepish. She passed the book she was holding to her mistress.

Without any hesitation Miss Esme gave it to AJ.

He flicked through its pages, then, somewhat disappointed, said, "It's a recipe book. There's nothing but recipes in it."

"That's a startling bit of observation," said Leon. "Ingleby showed me the book downstairs. Look at the flyleaf."

AJ looked again and then he saw it. Written in pencil were the words "The property of Miss Meacock, maid to the Bramwell family of Hammersmith, 1806." The writing was self-conscious and had been struck through with pen, and under it, in a clearer and bolder hand of the same author, was written "Mrs. Meacock, Housekeeper to Samuel Dalton, Esq., of Clerkenwell, 1810."

"Where did you find this?" AJ asked Agnes.

Agnes sounded defensive.

"Mrs. Meacock said it was her bible and she would not hesitate to fire anyone who touched it. Then she fired all the servants anyway with not a why or a wherefore of an explanation. I was boiling. Then she refused to give me a reference and without it I won't be able to find a respectable job. So to spite her, I nicked it. I never done nothing like it before, honest I haven't."

"I am glad you did," said Leon. He was still looking at Mrs. Meacock's writing. Then, closing the book, he stood up and said, "I think we need to go to Hammersmith and find out if the Bramwells have fond memories of their maid."

Ingleby thought it an excellent plan but advised them that due to the snow many roads were impassable and AJ and Leon should take the steam passage upriver to Hammersmith and, once there, inquire in the local inn for the Bramwell house.

"Can I come with you?" asked Miss Esme.

"That would be great," said AJ. He could spend more time in her company.

"Mr. Jobey," said Mrs. Ingleby, horrified at the idea. "Whatever are you suggesting?"

"Oh, no, I just I thought that . . ."

Ingleby wasn't interested in what AJ had in mind, but was adamant that Miss Esme shouldn't leave his house.

"That would be insane," he said. "She must stay here. The inquest will have reconvened, and we don't know who might be looking for Miss Esme in an hour's time."

At the word "insane" Miss Esme sank back into her chair.

"You are right, Mr. Ingleby," she said. "If the inquest finds that my father was poisoned then I suppose the suspect is either me or Mrs. Meacock."

"I doubt very much that you could kill flies, let alone poison your father or Baldwin," said Leon. "But without proof to the contrary, we are stuck."

AJ wanted to forget the social niceties and put his arms round her, to take the sadness from those gray eyes and color her life with hope, tell her he could carry her away to the future even though it might not be the brightest of Utopias.

He put on his hat and coat and followed Ingleby and Leon downstairs.

At the back door Ingleby said quietly, "If the coroner finds Miss Esme guilty, you know I will not be able to hide her here for long. The alternative would be the other side of Jobey's Door."

CHAPTER 40

The River Thames, a long snake of black, bloated water, wound through the great city, bursting with the waste of its citizens. Even in the bitter cold there was a smell to it, a smell that told Londoners they were home.

AJ and Leon caught the steam packet at Blackfriars, astonished to find the river so congested on such a bitter day. Vessels of every kind bobbed energetically about, the ferrymen taking their passengers across the river skimmed like dragonflies over the water, the wash of the steam packet rocking them so that they looked as if at any moment they would capsize with their precious cargo into that mercury liquid. Lumps of ice floated in this dark cocktail, a true witches' brew.

After Westminster, London gave way to countryside, and here both travelers could easily have forgotten the reason for their journey, so amazing was it to see the land naked of the endless peppering of high-rise buildings. No planes heading into Heathrow, just screeching gulls whirling white against the sky, sheep huddled together in frozen fields; a rural scene doomed to be buried in tarmac. By the time they reached

Hammersmith they could have been in another country and London could have been another world.

They were taken by the water ferryman to the Dove Inn. It had a fire blazing, and AJ ordered the dish of the day and two jugs of beer, and by degrees began to feel his fingers once more. The place was near deserted; the season being festive, many people were spending time with their families, and the innkeeper was genuinely pleased to greet two new customers. It did not take them long to find out that the Bramwells' house lay more towards Chiswick than Hammersmith and that to get there it would be best to take another water ferry.

The river, when seen from the vulnerable perspective of a waterman's boat, took on a truly menacing quality. The sun had tired of its efforts, and the snow-filled sky looked set to burst once more as the little boat wobbled to and fro before finally landing at the steps at Chiswick. They were in the heart of the countryside, the M4 but a glint in the eye of a future town planner. It was heartbreaking to see what progress would destroy: the still, snowy meadows and copses, doomed to be lost under miles of roads and ribboned houses, and the hot wheels of aeroplanes.

The Bramwell house was surrounded by tall railings in which was a gate that was firmly locked. The windows were barred, but apart from that the house looked not dissimilar to others thereabouts. The gate possessed a bell and AJ rang it. A servant in an apron came out. He had a serious face and didn't look as if he was expecting visitors.

"We have come to see Mr. Bramwell," said AJ.

There was a pause.

"Mr. Bramwell is long dead and buried."

"Then would it be possible to see the owner of the house?" said Leon. "It's a matter of some urgency, to do with a Miss Meacock who was once a maid here."

They were shown into a wood-paneled hall furnished with a collection of chairs and a table. It was Leon who noticed that the chairs and table were all screwed to the floor.

"Why do you think they did that?" asked AJ, but before Leon could answer a woman appeared.

Soberly dressed like the servant, she had an expression of concern on her face, as if her days were made up of perpetually saying, "There, there."

"How can I help you?" she asked.

"I wonder if you can tell me where we might find Mrs. Bramwell?" said AJ.

"My late husband was William Bramwell. I am his widow. My servant tells me that you have some interest in Martha Meacock."

Leon stepped forward and bowed.

"My name is Leon Grant and this is Mr. Jobey. We have serious suspicions about Martha Meacock and would like to ask you some questions. Mrs. Bramwell, I take it this is a mental health hospital?"

AJ looked at him, impressed.

"A lunatic asylum," said Mrs. Bramwell. "Although you, sir, have a kinder way of seeing these troubled souls. My late husband ran the asylum."

AJ had imagined a grand house on the river with servants'

quarters and a huge kitchen. Never had it occured to him it would turn out to be a nuthouse.

"And Miss Meacock was a maid here?" said AJ, not quite able to picture it."

"No, sir. She was an inpatient."

For a moment AJ and Leon could hardly believe what they had just heard.

"I think we should talk in the parlor," said Mrs. Bramwell, and she led them to a room where the furniture was not screwed to the floor.

"Martha Meacock," Mrs. Bramwell explained, "came from a respectable family. Her father was a clergyman and a widower. He had a son and a daughter. Reverend Meacock told us that at the age of twenty his daughter attempted to kill her brother. That was how she came to be committed here."

"So she was never a maid?" asked AJ.

"Yes, she was," said Mrs. Bramwell. "After five years her father died and there was no more money to pay for her upkeep. Her brother cared little if she went to the devil, as he put it in his letter to us. My husband believed many of his patients were not as insane as their families liked everyone to believe. He took pity on Martha, and rather than turn her out suggested we took her on as our maid. She was a bright, pleasant young woman and much taken with my husband. After a time she became a great help to him with his experiments."

That alarm bell rang again.

"What sort of experiments?" asked Leon.

"William was a chemist. His particular interest was in poisons, and he hoped to find a test that would show the existence of arsenic in a corpse, for it is impossible in many cases to be certain if someone has died of poison or some unknown malady. Many people have been wrongly accused of murder. Sadly, my husband was suddenly taken ill before he could complete his work. Martha left us shortly after he died. Such a kind woman she was, to whom life had not been kind."

"And you never saw anything strange in her behavior?" asked Leon.

"No," said Mrs. Bramwell.

AJ had detected a slight pause before she'd answered, and so had Leon.

"Mrs. Bramwell, the reason we are here," said Leon, "is because a young woman, the daughter of the late Samuel Dalton, is to be wrongly accused of murdering her father by arsenic poisoning. The housekeeper to the Dalton family is a Mrs. Martha Meacock."

Mrs. Bramwell was shocked.

"Are you positive it is the same woman?"

"Yes," said Leon, bringing out the recipe book for Mrs. Bramwell to see.

"That is certainly her writing." Tears filled her eyes. "Oh dear," she said. "My husband was such a gentle man, a trusting man; all he saw was the good in everyone. Martha, I believe, fell in love with him. We both thought it was a girlish infatuation, nothing more."

"Which—please forgive me asking—your husband didn't reciprocate?"

"No, no. In fact, he told me shortly before he was taken ill that he had come to the conclusion that he had misjudged the severity of Martha's mental condition."

⸻

The journey back was a very somber one. The nearer AJ and Leon came to Holborn, the more agitated AJ felt. Oh, for a mobile phone. The thought of the wine on Mrs. Furby's side table rattled him, for he now had a strong feeling that it might have been mad Martha Meacock who had sent it to Mrs. Renwick. She wouldn't want any tittle-tattle, and arsenic in Madeira wine would ultimately silence the most talkative of tongues.

CHAPTER 41

Mrs. Furby, along with the other boarders, was in the dining room when AJ burst in.

The Madeira wine was uncorked.

"Has anyone drunk the wine?" he cried.

He repeated the question again and again, and it took a while for him to hear exactly what Slim was saying.

No one had touched the wine because Slim wouldn't let them. "You can't just go drinking stuff when you don't know where it comes from. And the cork looked a bit dodgy."

AJ hugged him and collapsed on the carpet.

He woke to find himself in bed and Mrs. Renwick staring down at him declaring that he had a fever and that the doctor should be sent for as a matter of urgency.

"In my humble opinion," she said, "he needs to be bled."

"No, no," he said. "All I need is sleep."

Mrs. Renwick agreed that sleep would be very sensible indeed and insisted that he take one of her remedies at least.

Slim ushered Mrs. Renwick from the room. Leon stood at the end of the bed.

"I would say your leg's infected," he said. "You need to go to hospital and have your dressings changed. And I don't mean here."

"No way. Absolutely no way," said AJ. "Do you think I'm leaving now? Come on, bro, help me. When this is done, then I'll go back, I promise. I have to see Ingleby and tell him about mad Mrs. Meacock. And I need to find out who murdered my father."

"All right, calm it." Leon sat down beside AJ. "I think I've worked it out. Mrs. Meacock was obsessed by Mr. Bramwell. To her he seemed a father figure and lover wrapped in one. Except just like her father and her brother, he ultimately rejected her. With the logic of a raving psycho Miss Meacock calmly saw what needed to be done. She'd been a good student and she graduated with flying colors. Not only did she murder Mr. Bramwell, but she got away with it. Now, regarding your dad. Remember what Samuel Dalton said when he was dying? When he thought he was talking to your grandfather, Old Jobey? Think about it—Mrs. Meacock was Dalton's mistress. She would kill the Jobeys to keep his love. And I wouldn't be surprised if she made sure his wife ended her days in a loony bin. Not too tricky—after all, Martha Meacock was an expert in madness."

AJ tried to get out of bed.

"I'm going to see Mr. Stone now. There's no time to lose."

Slim came back with Mrs. Renwick's remedy.

"Drink up," he said.

"No," said AJ. "I have to . . ."

"Drink up," said Slim firmly. "Listen to me, AJ. You have two friends here who would do anything for you. The word you need to get acquainted with is 'delegate.' It means letting other people share the load. Drink, sleep. Mr. Flint knows this chemist, and we are about to take the wine to him to find out if it's been tampered with. Leon will go to Ingleby and together they'll see Mr. Stone. See what I mean? Delegate."

AJ drank the potion and sank onto the pillows.

He dreamed Mrs. Meacock was waiting for him in the shadows. Behind her stood the ghost of Samuel Dalton, blood running from his eyes and from his lips. All that was left of the ground floor of the house in St. John Street was the staircase. Mrs. Meacock and the ghost walked up it. AJ didn't want to follow them, but in nightmares you aren't given those kinds of choices. He saw the car park beneath him, and on the landing was a round table at which were seated four figures, each shrouded in white linen. Before them were broken plates, scattered cutlery, wineglasses knocked over, and a magpie walking about, squawking. Mrs. Meacock removed the linen cloth from each of the diners, a magic trick revealing the Jobey family dead and decaying. Bare feet hung above the table, and he looked up to see a human chandelier. In each of Annie Sorrell's hands was a candle. Horrorstruck, he tried to back away, forgetting there were no walls. He fell over the edge, down into feather blackness.

He woke, grateful for the daylight. The nightmare had convinced him. He would go to St. John Street and speak to Mrs. Meacock face to face.

"Mr. Jobey," said Mrs. Furby when she saw him in the dining room. "You shouldn't be up. Nellie, Nellie, go and fetch Mrs. Renwick."

"No," said AJ, and he meant it. "No, I'm all right. I just need some coffee. Stop fussing, all of you."

Leon and Slim watched him make a hash of trying to put on his coat.

"Wait," said Leon. "Don't you want to know what happened when Ingleby and me went to see Mr. Stone?"

"Yes," said AJ, one arm in his coat.

"I told Mr. Stone all we found out yesterday and he is asking the coroner to have the inquest into Mr. Dalton's death reopened until the body of William Bramwell can be exhumed and examined for arsenic poisoning."

"Great," said AJ. "But I want to see Mrs. Meacock. I want her to tell me herself that she poisoned my family."

"AJ, you're delirious," said Leon. "You need to go back—and you know where I mean."

"After I've seen Mrs. Meacock."

Slim suggested that the only thing to do was to take him by force to Ingleby's house.

"Hello?" said AJ. "I'm here in the room, you know. I can hear what you're saying."

"All right. I'll go with him," said Leon. "But she's as mad as a fish, bro—we should be mob-handed. Slim, you'd better find Ingleby and tell him to come to St. John Street straightaway."

CHAPTER 42

If it was cold that day or colder than the day before, AJ, warmed by fever, didn't notice. The house at St. John Street looked deserted, but Leon spotted a vertical beam of light down the edge of the doorframe. Someone hadn't properly shut it. He helped AJ up the two stone steps and pushed the door open.

"Samuel?" called a faint voice from an upstairs room. "Is that you, Samuel, my dear one?"

Cautiously, AJ and Leon went up towards the voice.

"William, my love?" it called again.

As AJ and Leon reached the room from where the voice came, the front door slammed, and for a moment, just one moment, AJ felt as if the lid of his coffin had been nailed down. On the first-floor landing, light slipped out of what AJ remembered as Mr. Dalton's bedroom.

"Hello?" he called, a tad shakily.

"Samuel? I'm dying, Samuel. I drank my own medicine just as you told me to. I am going to hell. You said I would."

The bedchamber was ablaze with candles, yet still they were defeated by the gloom. The cold felt thick. He could see his breath wispy in front of him. Most of the furnishings were gone, leaving only the draped four-poster bed where Mr. Dalton had died, and near the empty grate a footstool and a hard-backed wooden chair heaped with clothes. AJ thought he had made a mistake, that no one was in the room, until the heap of clothes spoke.

"Is that you, William? Do you forgive your little Martha?" it said.

There sat a nightmare of a woman, her lips blistered, her eyes sunk into the hollow sockets of her skull, her voice no more than the grating of sandpaper. She looked as near dead as a living person could, her skin puce, stretched tight across her face.

"Holy shit," said Leon from the door. "She looks as if she's escaped from a horror film."

She stirred and put out a hand to AJ.

"Martha Meacock?" he said, uncertain.

"Yes," she said. "Martha Meacock as ever was. My eyesight is failing me—is that you, Young Jobey?"

"Yes, it's me."

"Young Jobey, stole the girl, now come to judge me, to send me to the gallows. But I'm not going to hang like Annie Sorrell. No one will see me rise on the rope."

In the street a dog howled.

"Hear that?" she said. "Hell is waiting for me. My enemies gather to watch my suffering, to gloat at my agony. But they won't see me hang, no, they won't see me rise on the rope. Sit, sit beside me."

Reluctantly AJ pulled up the stool and sat as far away from her as he could.

"Nearer," she said.

He moved a little closer.

"Can you see them?" she asked.

"Who?"

"They are all in this chamber. Over there is your father—he stands by the window."

AJ could see nothing in the flickering candlelight but an empty room.

"There is Annie Sorrell . . . there Old Jobey . . . there your aunt . . . and there my sweet William, who I loved."

Even with a fever AJ could see nothing.

"Samuel betrayed me," she whispered. She licked her lips, her mouth open. "He changed his will . . . after he promised me . . . after all I did for him . . ." Mrs. Meacock sat back in her chair. A look of terror came over her face. Even Leon was beginning to be spooked out by a room full of nothing.

"Samuel—he is here too."

"Where?" asked AJ.

"In the bed. He is there, sitting upright . . . he is staring at me. Stop him staring at me, Young Jobey."

AJ looked at the bed. It was empty. Her hand wildly shot out and grabbed at AJ's coat.

"He didn't keep his promise to me . . . he altered the will. That man there—he altered the will."

"Which man, Mrs. Meacock?"

"Mr. Baldwin," she said. "He was the first to arrive today. He has come to see me die. 'Dear Mrs. Meacock,' he says, 'dear Mrs. Meacock.' Pompous prick.

*"Mad Martha Meacock
The clergyman's daughter
Soaked the flypaper
In water*

"It is he you should blame for your family's murder. He would have killed you too. I should have let him."

"Me? Why?"

"Why? Why?" she screeched. "Mr. Baldwin played me for a fool. It was he . . . he who told me Samuel wanted rid of Old Jobey and his son. I loved Samuel so much . . . I bought a magpie . . . in Clerkenwell . . . hired a street urchin to carry the cage . . . it was so easy. Frightened Annie Sorrell witless . . . gave the urchin a sweet for his troubles . . . watched him drown in the Fleet. When she swung at the gallows I told Samuel . . . told him what I'd done for him, the proof of my love. He called me mad. And Mrs. Dalton kept the bastard." Her voice changed to something altogether sweeter. "Bring me that box."

AJ hadn't noticed it before. It was on the floor, a plain wooden box. He handed it to her and she opened it.

"His papers," said Mrs. Meacock. "All for snuffboxes."

The hollowed-eyed skeleton rose from her chair, laughing. Leon moved towards her and she dropped the box.

"Who are you?" she shouted, knocking over a candle. It rolled across the floor, catching on the curtain, which flared up in a screen of flames. AJ thought he saw a man standing in them, his eyes dark, his face like his own. He was smiling at him.

"Tell him, Mr. Baldwin," rasped Mrs. Meacock over the sound

243

of the burning curtains. "Tell him what you did. He won't . . . he can't. Mr. Baldwin came to dine . . . to change the will . . . he wanted something sweet and salty to give to you. I gave him it in his wine . . . sent him packing with household flour." She made a sound that crackled at the back of her throat. "A slow death . . ."

AJ could hear Ingleby's voice and banging on the front door.

"AJ? We need to get out of here now, bro," said Leon.

"The box—take the box," said AJ.

Leon picked it up and ran down the stairs to let in Ingleby and Slim.

Mrs. Meacock rose from her seat and caught hold of a candle, and before AJ could stop her she had thrown it on the bed.

"There, Samuel!" she screamed. "See how much I loved you!"

The room was dancing with flames.

"Don't tell them where we are," said Mrs. Meacock. She clutched AJ's wrist and pulled him towards her. "They must not find me, they must not."

Ingleby stood filling the doorway, Leon and Slim behind him.

"Leave this to me," he said.

Mrs. Meacock, flames nibbling at her clothes, held tight to AJ. With one mighty push Ingleby freed him. Mrs. Meacock fell back into her chair, near engulfed in fire.

Ingleby thew AJ over his shoulder. As they left the burning house Mrs. Meacock's voice trailed after them.

> *"Mad Martha Meacock*
> *The clergyman's daughter.*
> *Liked to put arsenic*
> *In the water."*

CHAPTER 43

In the hall of Mr. Ingleby's house the face above the front door peered down at AJ as he sat on a chair holding the box, the smell of singed wool wafting around him. He saw in the shadows Leon and Slim deep in conversation with Ingleby. They hadn't noticed, or perhaps he had imagined, Miss Esme standing beside him, her hand on his shoulder. Her words sounded as if they were coming from the depths of the ocean.

They were talking about him as if he wasn't there.

Leon said, "It's simple, I'll take him back."

"No," said Slim. "What happens if the feds pick you up? I'll do it."

AJ struggled to his feet.

"No one need come with me. I'm perfectly capable of going by myself," he said, and toppled forward, to be caught by Ingleby.

"We should call a doctor," Ingleby said.

"What—and have him lose a leg?" said Leon.

"Come on," said Slim. "We'd better make a move."

"You're not coming with me, bro. I can do it alone."

Miss Esme suddenly spoke. "I will go with Mr. Jobey," she said, "and make sure he returns home safely."

AJ had his hand on the doorknob. Miss Esme was beside him, and before he knew it she had pulled the door open. For one moment the alien noise of the twenty-first century clattered into the hall and they stood together on the threshold between the lines of time. Miss Esme stepped over it and AJ followed, closing the door behind them.

Miss Esme stopped and looked around her. A wet afternoon was steadily being overtaken by night.

"Where are we?"

If ever a question was an elephant then that question was it, thought AJ.

"In the twenty-first century," he said. "In a car park."

A car park is a complicated thing to explain to someone who's never seen a car; a derelict car park even more so.

"Monstrous metal and an orchestra of unknown sounds. This is a strange new world indeed," she said. "The door has gone."

AJ knew he should be her guide, but the trouble was he hadn't the strength to climb over the car park fence. He hoped that someone might come in through the gate and he would be able to sneak them both out. Unfortunately his leg wasn't in on the plan, and even with Esme's help he fell over twice and thought he had dropped the box only to find Esme holding it as she might a shield. He became aware of a dog barking, blue lights flashing—again—and electronic noise exploding around him. Where's the drama, he thought, what's on fire?

Esme put her hands to her ears.

"Is all the world as broken and destroyed as this?" she said.

AJ was definitely losing the plot. It slowly dawned in his

befuddled mind that the lights, the dogs and the police might all be there for another reason.

"Stay put, you two," said a voice attached to the end of a torch that was shining straight at him. "You're under arrest."

"It's all right," said AJ to Esme as the policeman clapped handcuffs on him.

He heard Esme say, "Take your hands off me, sir! You are not a gentleman."

Then AJ lost his grip on the here and now completely and everything fizzed round the edge of his vision into blackout.

He came to, aware only of an oblong lozenge of light glaring down at him from the ceiling of a windowless cubicle. A nurse was folding his clothes.

"Where am I?" said AJ.

A doctor walked in.

"Royal London A&E," she said, picking up the chart from the end of his bed. "How're you feeling?"

"Odd. Slightly time-worn," said AJ.

Then he remembered in a lightning flash: Esme.

"My friend. I was with a friend," he said desperately. "A girl. Is she here? Where is she?"

"Can you tell me your name?" said the doctor.

"AJ . . . Aiden Jobey."

"Do you have any relatives we can contact?"

AJ gave Elsie's number.

"Where's my friend?" he asked again. "Her name's Esme."

Had he been hallucinating? Had he imagined that Esme had come through the door with him?

"A girl," he said again. "A girl called Esme was with me."

The doctor went away and came back with a tray of needles.

"Why didn't you keep your hospital appointment, Aiden?" she asked. "The wound in your leg is infected."

"I was busy." AJ could see that didn't go down too well. He corrected himself. "I lost track of time. Please—could you find out where Esme is?"

"It's been a long night," said the doctor.

She stuck the butterfly needle in the back of his hand and put up a drip.

"Have you been to a fancy-dress party?" asked the doctor.

"Yes," said AJ.

At least that explained the clothes.

"Where was this party?"

She didn't look at him, seeming more concerned with the health of his chart.

"I can't remember."

"Have you taken any drugs?"

"No."

"Are you on any medication?"

"No."

"Have you been drinking?"

"No, no, no. Just tell me—where is Esme?"

CHAPTER 44

Once you enter the hospital system you are on a different planet whether you like it or not.

"You'll be going up to the ward soon," said the doctor, clipping the chart to the end of the bed.

"No," said AJ. "I need to find my friend."

"Not tonight. You're staying here."

A policeman of a sunny disposition followed the nurse and the porter who wheeled AJ to the ward.

Lying he had never found easy, but from a hospital bed it wasn't as tricky. Nearly all the work was done for him by the policeman.

"You were at a fancy-dress party, is that right?"

AJ nodded.

"And I suppose your mates thought it would be a laugh if they left you on the wrong side of the car park fence?"

"Yeah, something like that," said AJ. "Could you tell me where my friend Esme is?"

"She is being held at Holborn police station until we can make some sense of what she's saying. Do you know what drugs she's taken? Or who her family is?"

AJ sighed.

"Yeah, her grandmother is Elsie Tapper and her father is Norris Tapper. They live at Bodman House in Stoke Newington. I gave the doctor Mrs. Tapper's phone number."

"Your friend says her father's name is Dalton."

Damn, thought AJ. If only he'd had time to tell her about her real parents, to prepare her for the electronic jungle. His mind filled with the vision of Elsie and Norris going to the police station and Esme saying she hadn't a clue who they were.

"Are you employed?"

"Yes. I'm a clerk at Baldwin Groat, in Gray's Inn."

He realized that in the eyes of the police officer he had suddenly risen from the pile of hopeless youth. He was somebody. He was a clerk in legal chambers.

In the end he was cautioned and told to report to the station in five days' time. After that he fell fast asleep.

AJ slept for two days solid. The nurse told him he'd had visitors, his mum and his auntie, but hadn't woken up. On the third day, he was told that he could go home. New Year was a busy time and his bed was needed. Norris turned up with a carrier bag. At first AJ didn't recognize him. He looked . . . solid, content. His hair was cut short and he was clean-shaven, but the main difference was the beaming smile that went from one ear to the other.

"Happy New Year. How're you feeling, mate?" he asked.

"Wobbly," said AJ. "But otherwise all right."

"You're as white as a wedding dress."

"Did you find Esme?"

"Who?" said Norris.

"Oh no," said AJ, putting his hands to his head. "No, no, don't tell me you didn't find her. Bugger it! I shouldn't have slept so long. God knows where she is now . . ."

Norris burst out laughing.

"Of course we found her!"

AJ let out a huge sigh.

"What happened?"

"The police assumed she'd taken drugs or been on the booze. I thought it might be tricky trying to explain, but turns out, Ingleby, bless him, had told her about me and Annie. Anyway, you know the funny thing? They say blood is thicker than water, and the minute I saw her and she saw me and Mum, she smiled such a lovely smile. Mum gave her a big hug and whispered to her to stay quiet and we'd have her out in a jiffy, and we did." Norris handed AJ the carrier bag. "Here, put these on. I thought you'd look a right nob walking about in nineteenth-century gear."

"How is Esme finding this London?"

"Duck to water, father to daughter. Never meant to be anywhere else, just like her old dad. This is her century, the other was a huge mistake. She's trying to get her head round it all. Now, come on, let's get out of here. I can't stand hospitals. They give me the heebie-jeebies."

Outside, he hailed a cab.

"Shouldn't we take the bus?" said AJ.

"No," said Norris. "Stokey, mate," he said to the cabbie. "Bloody luxury. You know, I was going to be a cabbie before I followed your dad."

"What was he like—my dad?"

251

"Lucas Jobey? A wild card—clever and too kindhearted for his own good. I tell you this: he loved your mum, and what happened to him and to Annie has cast a long shadow over all our lives. Loss is a very hard thing to deal with. Loss has lead weights attached to it."

At Bodman House, Norris walked behind AJ, carrying his things as he slowly climbed the stairs. He heard footsteps coming down and looked up. A girl he had never seen before stood on the first-floor landing shyly smiling at him. She had short, bobbed hair and was dressed in jeans and a sweatshirt. He was thinking, she's cool, when to his surprise this unknown person took his arm.

"Mr. Jobe— AJ," she said. "You're home."

"Miss . . . Esme?" he said.

"Yes," she said, smiling. "Who did you think it was?"

CHAPTER 45

Elsie came out of the kitchen wearing her Christmas apron that had on it a huge face of a reindeer with a red nose.

"Good to see you, love," she said, giving AJ a kiss. "And thank you for sending these two home."

"Best quiz night ever, wasn't it, Mum?"

Elsie giggled in a way that AJ had never heard before.

"I've made lunch," she said. She dropped her voice to a whisper. "Your mum's here. Roxy's gone off with a group of friends to the cinema, so it's just us. Oh—and by the way, your mum knows everything. Norris told her."

"Really? You mean about the door?"

"Yes," said Elsie. "And about the murder of your dad. Knocked her for six, that did. But she's been a real help. She took Esme off to the Angel and sorted her out some clothes. Be nice, love."

Jan was standing by the Christmas tree in the lounge.

"Give us a hug, then," she said.

This is a first, thought AJ, hugging her. He couldn't remember the last time such a thing had happened.

"All Esme and me want to know," said Jan, "is that you aren't going go back and stay there."

"Where?"

"Where your dad went."

AJ had been trying not to think about what he was going to do. A wail from the eternal electronic jungle whirled up Church Street, and it was then that he knew that this was his city. He knew the beat, he knew the hum of home, he knew this was his time.

"No, Mum, I'm not, but—" He stopped. "Why did you never tell me about him?"

Jan brushed down her dress as if invisible fluff was stuck to it.

"Go on, Jan," said Norris, handing her a Babycham. "Go on, tell him. Sit down, mate, you have to rest that leg."

There was a strangled silence.

"There's nothing to tell," said Jan.

Elsie came in with a plate of cheese straws and sat on the sofa. Esme quietly sat down beside her.

"Jan, love," said Elsie firmly. "You can't run out of petrol before you've even put the car in first gear. Start it up, girl."

Jan bit her bottom lip and then said so quietly that AJ wasn't sure he'd heard her, "I loved your dad. To tell you the truth, I've never loved anyone like I loved him. He was all the lights on the Christmas tree—but brighter, if you know what I mean." She sniffed. "We were married and I'd never been so happy. You know, I thought I was the luckiest girl in the whole of this block of flats—in the whole damn world. Lucas said he had to do one last thing and then he would be back for good, no more traveling. I thought he meant he was going to find another job. I thought we'd be together until we were two old wrinklies."

"What did you think he did?" asked AJ.

"He said he was a traveling salesman," said Jan.

Norris laughed. "Well, that's one way of putting it."

"Your dad told me about the door that led to where," said Jan, "and I thought it was just one of his fantastical stories. He had such wonderful stories in him, he made the past come to life. I didn't realize the past was alive and ticking, that he was a time traveler." She let out a noise that AJ put down as a laugh. "Me—Jan Flynn—marry a time traveler? Come on, that only happens in films or in *Doctor Who*. I'm just an ordinary person, nothing special, nothing to walk through a door for. When he never came back I thought I would break in two. Then there was you. I didn't know I was pregnant when he left. You were the only thing that kept me stuck together. You looked so like him, it hurt. I thought the rat had abandoned us, taken away my future and left me with nothing but a baby. Elsie always said there was more to it, but by the time I realized I would never see him again, all the anger that had been churning in me had set like cement. What is it you call me?" She paused to think. "That's it—the red reptile. I found the notebook in your room. It made me laugh. 'The Red Reptile Handling Manual.' I thought, I deserve that."

"Mum, you shouldn't go nosing about."

"And neither should you, but you have."

"If he hadn't," said Elsie, "I would never have had the best Christmas of my life. I would never have had my Norris back and never"—she gave Esme a cuddle—"met my granddaughter."

CHAPTER 46

Norris and AJ were barred from helping with the washing-up; AJ on account of his leg, which was now propped up on a stool, and Norris because his mum was spoiling him something rotten. Esme joined them; there wasn't space in the kitchen for three people. AJ looked at Norris and Esme sitting together and thought it was hard to imagine them in any other period of time.

"I've got to ask," said AJ. "What happened when you showed up at the Rose and Crown?"

"My mum got to her feet, clipped me round the ear and said—pardon my French—"Where the hell have you been?" Then she burst into tears."

AJ laughed. "I wish I'd been there."

Elsie and Jan were having a good old natter in the kitchen; they could even be heard giggling.

"What exactly did my father do?" asked AJ.

"He traded with the future is what he did," said Norris. "He brought snuffboxes through the door."

"What snuffboxes?" said Jan, coming in with a tray of coffee. "You never told me anything about snuffboxes."

"You never asked," said Norris. "They were little gems, worth a bloody fortune."

"You mean those three little boxes I've got in my knicker drawer are worth something?"

"Three of them?" said Norris. "Bloody hell, Jan, you could have been living in a palace. You still got them?"

"Of course I have. Lucas gave them to me on our wedding day. He said nothing about them being worth a bloody fortune. I thought they were just pretty trinkets."

"Jan, girl, you are well set."

"Stop it," said Jan. "You're winding me up."

"I'm not. The prices those little charmers fetched at auction eighteen years ago blew my mind. Lord knows what they would be worth today."

"Is that what Baldwin was up to?" asked Jan.

"Yeah, sort of. He had his greedy fat fingers in lots of grubby little pies."

"Hold on," said AJ. "How did my dad meet Baldwin?"

"Through Old Jobey. It was the old boy who first went through the door. The trouble was, he never suited the twentieth century—too stuck in the mud of his own time. He had a temper when he was off the lead and would bark at anyone who crossed him. It didn't take long before he needed a lawyer in this century—I mean, the last one. His lawyers, Stone Groat, had been in Gray's Inn, so he went there and found Baldwin Groat. He liked lawyers, did Old Jobey, and Baldwin liked nutters, especially rich nutters. After a while Old Jobey didn't want to come this way anymore. His health was failing, so he sent Samuel Dalton with the snuffboxes." Esme moved a little closer to Norris. "Baldwin and Dalton would meet for a pint in the Apple Tree at Mount Pleasant, the goods would change hands and Dalton would return to Old Jobey carrying gold. It was only when Lucas took over from Dalton that he realized exactly how much Dalton and Baldwin had been ripping him off."

"That was when I met your dad," said Jan. "I was working in the chambers as a tea girl and cleaner. I never liked Baldwin—he was a smarmy git, always trying to touch me up. Today it has a name."

"It had a name then," said Norris. "Bloody bastard."

"Lucas met Norris through me," continued Jan.

"Yeah," said Norris. "He told me about the door in dribs and drabs. I didn't know what to think. He told me he didn't trust Baldwin but couldn't persuade his father to cut his ties with him as he had with Dalton. I introduced Lucas to a mate of mine who'd done time with me at Feltham."

"Taking and driving, naughty boy," shouted Elsie, who was earwigging from the kitchen.

"This mate had been to Eton, had posh friends and by then owned an antiques shop in Notting Hill Gate."

"What had he been in prison for?" asked AJ.

"He was a thief," said Norris. "All delicate fingers and pink ties, that boy. He could hardly believe what he was seeing when I took Lucas along to show him the goods. He thought at first they must be fakes. He soon found out they were the real McCoy. Anyway, to cut a long story short, Lucas and he did a deal both were happy with. Baldwin took it badly, said he had a contract with Old Jobey giving him exclusive rights over the trade in snuffboxes. By that time, I'd been through the door with Lucas a few times and met Annie. I had a mind to bring Annie here . . ." Norris paused for a moment and Esme slipped her arm through his. "When Lucas told his old man how much gold Dalton and Baldwin had stolen from him over the years, it got ugly. Old Jobey went berserk and decided the door should be locked so no one else could profit from his business. He made up his mind that he wanted his son home. Lucas had other plans. He wanted to lock the door too, and stay in the twentieth century with Jan. The trouble was, the key had gone missing. I had my suspicions that Baldwin nicked it."

"Then Baldwin had my family murdered," said AJ. "And with the Jobeys out of the way and the door unlocked, he and Dalton were free to carry on the trade until . . . until . . ." The pinball machine stuttered back into life. "What was the name of that mate of yours?"

"Purcell," said Norris.

"David Purcell?" said AJ. "You sure?"

"Certain. I was thinking I might look him up."

"So Dalton and Baldwin hooked up with Purcell," said AJ.

"I don't know about that," said Norris. "I was away at the time."

"Here's something I don't understand," said AJ. "Baldwin was looking for the key. If he'd nicked it, he'd have known where it was."

"Not necessarily," said Jan. "Lucas took the key everywhere with him. He told me it was his talisman. Early one morning after Lucas disappeared, I found the key on Baldwin's desk. I was so upset, seeing it there, I put it in my pocket."

"Bloody hell, Jan, I wouldn't have thought you'd have it in you to do such a thing."

Jan giggled. "You don't get to be an old fighter without some cunning. I didn't know what to do with the key. I kept it for ages. In the end I gave it for safekeeping to a funny old geezer—a professor of history or something—who lived upstairs at Raymond Buildings. He'd been really kind to me. I took AJ to him when he was just a few weeks old."

Elsie came in with half a Christmas cake.

"*Casablanca*'s on the telly tonight. I love that film," she said, sucking her dentures. "I want to be swept off my feet and say, "Play it again, Sam." But with a Swedish accent."

CHAPTER 47

AJ spent his time recovering at his mum's flat. He had wondered how long her good mood would last. It could only be twenty-four hours—forty-eight at the most—before the red reptile raised its ugly head again. He was genuinely shocked when after three days she was still cheerful.

"You all right?" he asked her.

"Never better," said Jan. "I feel I've been given a new start. You don't think I've left it too late, do you?"

"No," said AJ. "It's never too late."

Even Roxy, to whom AJ couldn't claim to ever have felt close, now seemed to spend most of her time in his bedroom showing him YouTube videos that she thought he might find funny. AJ suspected the real reason for Roxy's newfound sisterly love was more to do with Esme than him.

He wondered if Esme could even be the cause of his mum's improved mood. She had a way about her that was calm. She listened to all everyone said, which was something that no one usually had time for. AJ had worked out that about a quarter of all conversation went unheard. If he had a hat he would take it off to Esme, for she was coping with this new world amazingly well. He kept trying and failing to put himself in her shoes. Supposing he walked into the year 2107—what would it look like? Would there still *be* a world? He reckoned it was easier by far to travel back in time than forward.

"At least," he said to Esme, "going back has some travel guides in the form of history books and the advantage of knowing what happened before it happens."

Once he hobbled into the kitchen to find her sitting on the floor staring at the washing machine on a spin cycle.

"OK?" he asked.

"Yes," she said, not looking at him. "Who would believe that a future world would be so full of magic?"

"It's a washing machine."

"It's fantastical."

"So was 1830," he said.

AJ's leg was better and he could walk without his crutches. He was hobbling round the flat when the midday news came on the TV.

Roxy was about to change the channel when AJ said, "Leave it on a sec."

Roxy sighed.

Ms. Finch was outside the Old Bailey, talking about the forgery case. So much had happened that AJ had forgotten about the box of papers that Esme had carried back. He went into his room and pulled it out from under his bed. Inside were meticulous handwritten documents relating to the purchase of the snuffboxes.

He put on his coat and picked up the box.

"I'm just going out. I won't be long."

"Mum will be furious," said Roxy.

He decided to get off the bus at Mount Pleasant. He walked to Phoenix Place and looked longingly through the wire mesh fence. He thought of Slim and Leon. He had to go back just once more to make sure they were all right.

Who am I kidding? he thought. If they don't want to be there they can walk through the door. There was nothing to stop them.

"AJ," said a voice. He turned to see the professor walking towards him. "Long time no see," he said. "It looks like you've been in the wars again."

"It's nothing," said AJ.

"Do you still have the key?"

AJ nodded.

"You haven't locked the door?"

"No."

"Going to?"

AJ laughed.

"Would it make a great difference if I did?"

"Jack chopped down the beanstalk," said the professor. "Killed the giant and that was that. I suppose if he hadn't, he might have had endless problems. Did you find what you were looking for?"

AJ hadn't thought he was looking for anything.

"I don't know," he said. "I found out what happened to my father."

"Are you going to Gray's Inn?"

"Yes."

"Then let me walk with you."

At the gates to Gray's Inn, where the whole adventure had begun, AJ said, "I'm going to go back and say goodbye."

"Time to close the door?" said the professor. "That's the right thing to do. The past is the past, and you, AJ, belong here."

"Where do you belong?"

"Now, that would be telling. Goodbye, AJ."

AJ waited in the hope of watching him walk away, but the professor seemed to dissolve into the city.

Chambers was just the same. AJ felt that he had been gone for centuries and was older and wiser because of it. Morton was in his office, his phone stuck to his ear as usual.

"Maurice, can I call you back later?" he said, seeing AJ in the doorway. "Aiden, what are you doing here? I wasn't expecting you until next week."

AJ put the box on Morton's desk.

"What's this?" said Morton.

"I think it's what Ms. Finch needs to win the Purcell case."

Morton took out the documents.

"Where did you find these?"

"They're what Mr. Baldwin was waiting for."

"Come on," said Morton, grabbing his coat.

Ms. Finch was cross-examining an expert witness for the prosecution who was convinced that the snuffboxes were forgeries of an extraordinarily professional nature. AJ and Morton bowed to the bench and AJ watched Morton take a seat behind Ms. Finch and pass her a note.

"May I approach the bench, Your Honor?"

"Yes, Counsel?" said the judge. "No one else from your chambers has been taken ill, I hope?"

"No, Your Honor. But documents have come to light that prove the snuffboxes are authentic. I would like to submit them as evidence."

There was an explosion of chattering in the court.

"Silence," said the judge. "I will see counsels in my chambers."

Morton, AJ and Ms. Finch sat in the canteen at the Old Bailey.

"Where did you find the papers?" asked Ms. Finch.

"They arrived this morning," said Morton. "Sent anonymously."

"Morton," said Ms. Finch. "I don't think you are telling the whole truth."

"I am being economical with it, Ms. Finch. But I have no doubt that you will find the documentation is in order."

"If it is, I think we will have won this case," said Ms. Finch. "It's good to see you, Aiden. When will you be back at work?"

"Next week," said AJ.

It was raining when Morton and AJ returned to Gray's Inn.

"I'll see you on Monday," said AJ.

"You don't escape so easily," said Morton. "My office."

Morton closed his door.

"Perhaps you would like to tell me where you found the papers."

"If I did you wouldn't believe me."

"Why don't you try me?" said Morton.

"Mr. Baldwin told me where to look. That evening I went to the London Clinic. He swore me to secrecy, so I can't tell you where they were. He was very keen to protect his reputation."

"I bet he was," said Morton quietly. "I always thought he was up to his neck in this forgery case. Well done, Aiden. I appreciate your discretion."

CHAPTER 48

AJ told Elsie he had to make sure that Leon and Slim didn't want to come back to the twenty-first century before he locked the door for good.

"Why would they, love?" she said. "What have they to come back for?"

AJ wanted to say, Come back for me.

Instead he said, "Because people will start asking questions."

"No, they won't," said Elsie. "I know this is hard for you, love. They are your best friends, you grew up together. The Three Musketeers, that's how I thought of you. But given my knowledge of life on the spin cycle, I would say they are better off where they are. Slim needs a woman a little older than him, and he needs a home, and by the sound of it this Mrs. Furball is just the ticket."

"Mrs. Furby," said AJ, laughing.

"And as for Leon, I always had a soft spot for him. Lovely lad. That letter he left me made me cry, it did. He said the only place he had ever felt safe as a kid was in my flat." Elsie had tears in her eyes. "I wish I could have done more for him.

Much as it breaks my old heart to think I won't see those two again, I know deep down they are better off there than here."

"I can't accept it," AJ said. "I just can't. They're my brothers."

"Come here and give your Auntie Elsie a hug. I think we should all go out tonight and have a meal at the Rose and Crown, make an occasion of it as we missed New Year's Eve."

"I just want to leave, Auntie Elsie—no fuss."

But once Elsie had her mind set on it, there was no way out.

To AJ it felt more like a wake than a celebration. No one had been happy to hear what he was planning to do.

Mum looked teary and Roxy looked bored. Norris sat morosely nursing his beer.

"This is cheerful," said AJ.

Jan said, "I don't think you should go. What if you never come back, like Lucas?"

"I agree," said Norris. "Think yourself lucky that you got out of there alive, mate. Anyway, what about the police station and your hospital appointment?"

"I've been to the police. And I'm not planning to stay there long," said AJ.

He caught Esme's eye. She was wearing a 1950s lace blouse that Elsie had given her. "Peachy" was how Norris had described her. AJ began to wonder if he was doing the right thing.

He stood up. "Another round?"

It was while AJ was getting the drinks that he saw Mr. Toker outside the pub. AJ had rather hoped he wouldn't see him.

"AJ," called Mr. Toker, waving to him. "How's the job going?"

"Fine, thanks," said AJ. He went out to speak to him.

"Have you seen my nephew at all?" asked Mr. Toker.

"No," said AJ, lying butterflies flapping in his stomach.

Mr. Toker sighed. "Up to no good somewhere, I suppose. It's a pity—he had potential. No doubt he'll turn up in court. I heard they busted Dr. Jinx and that the police want to question your friend Leon."

"Good," said AJ. "I mean, not about Leon, but about Jinx."

"Well, Sarah will be wondering where I am. I'd better be off."

"Happy New Year to you, Mr. Toker," said AJ.

Suddenly he knew he couldn't play happy-clappy families. He needed time to think about what he was about to do. He paid and asked the girl behind the bar if she wouldn't mind taking the drinks over to his table as he had to go out for a breath of air.

He stood on the steps of the pub, looking at the town hall. Was he doing the right thing? Could he live with himself if he didn't go back through the door? His two best friends in the world were there, and if he locked the door he would never see them again. That would be it, forever. No Slim, no Leon, just AJ.

"Are you quite well, AJ?"

He turned round and smiled at Esme.

"I just needed some air."

And without thinking he took her hand.

The sky glowed London orange. They crossed the road, walked through the alleyway at the side of the churchyard to the broken park gates and squeezed through.

They sat on the edge of the skate park, their feet dangling.

"Have you thought that you might want to go back?" said AJ.

What if she said yes she did? A barren landscape rose before him, a Nevada desert of grief.

"AJ, here young women are not confined by corsets and social etiquette. Here I can make something of myself and not be some man's chattel. I think Dad is right. I was born in the wrong century."

He felt that tug again.

"Esme, I don't think I can do it. I can't just say goodbye to Leon and Slim, lock the door and post the key through the letter box."

"Look at it a different way," said Esme. "You have given each of us a freedom we never would have had without you and the door."

AJ shook his head. The only thing that made this conversation bearable was the closeness of her, the smell of her.

"Yes. You have," she said quietly. "It's a new start. What do you call it? A reset. Against the odds you have reset our lives." She squeezed his hand. "Please come back. You don't belong on the other side."

"I will," he said. "I promise."

"It's a new year," Esme said. "A new future."

"A new start," said AJ. "For you and for me."

And then he kissed her.

CHAPTER 49

Norris insisted on going with AJ to Phoenix Place and Elsie insisted on going with Norris to make sure he came home.

"Why don't we invite the circus?" suggested AJ. "I mean, it's hard enough to break into the car park without all of you determined to draw attention to me."

Jan decided to stay behind with Esme.

"Remember," she said, taking hold of his hand. "Remember which side of the door your bread is buttered."

Now here he was, squashed between Norris and Elsie in the back of a minicab.

"You've got your medicine, love?" Elsie asked. "And your hat?"

"Yep."

AJ was already dressed in the nineteenth-century clothes he'd been wearing when he was taken to hospital.

"Three days, that's the maximum, and then you must be back," she said.

"Otherwise I'll turn into a pumpkin."

"Are you sure I shouldn't come?" said Norris for the fiftieth time.

"Certain," said AJ.

The taxi dropped them at the Mount Pleasant sorting office.

AJ didn't know quite what his next move was, but the idea of trailing Norris and Elsie in his wake definitely wasn't a part of it.

"Go home, please," he said. "I didn't want you to come in the first place."

"Don't move, either of you," said Elsie.

She straightened her woolly hat and waited. For what, AJ hadn't a clue. At last, a man walked up to the pedestrian gate to the car park. Elsie was off. She stood right behind him as he tapped in the code.

"Excuse me," she said as the gate swung open. The man jumped. "Sorry, love, I didn't mean to give you a fright. Can you help me? Am I going in the right direction for Islington?"

"It's that way," said the man. "Once you cross Farringdon Road there's a bus stop."

He pointed past Norris and AJ, who were looking as if they were nothing to do with Elsie. The man let himself in and closed the gate firmly behind him. Elsie walked back to where AJ and Norris were waiting.

"Come on," she said. "Let's get a cuppa."

"What was all that in aid of, Mum?" asked Norris as they walked to the café AJ had gone to with the professor.

"A pot of tea and three doughnuts, love," said Elsie to the waitress, sitting down.

"There's no time for this," said AJ.

"Sit down," said Elsie firmly.

Tea and three tired doughnuts were brought to them.

"I can't stay—"

"First," said Elsie, "let's find out the code for the gate."

"What?" said AJ.

"I won it at the Rose and Crown Quiz Night," she said. "It's a spy camera. I put it on my woolly hat. Now . . ." She played back the recording. "5621."

"That's genius," said AJ. "Just genius."

"That's me, love," said Elsie. "Well, you'd better be off. If there's a problem we'll be here for a bit. Good luck."

AJ walked towards the dried-up buddleia root on the wall. He knew it was the last time. After this visit he would lock the door and walk away, the past and the future forever divided. He felt strangely excited by the idea. He hoped that by now Slim and Leon would be missing the electronic jungle. To leave his two best friends behind would be to accept they were dead, and he couldn't do that.

Now he waited impatiently, eager to see them. Slowly the car park disappeared, and finally through the fog the door emerged. The Janus face stared down at him with its usual blank expression.

The hall, even in the middle of the day, was as dark as if it were night. Dust-filled sunlight thieved through the fanlight to reveal His Honor sitting on the balustrade, the tips of his feathers gleaming neon white, his head at such an angle that it looked as if he had been waiting for him. AJ took off his hat and bowed to the bird, a mark of respect. One for sorrow.

"Mr. Jobey, is that you?" Ingleby came down the stairs. "What are you doing here?"

"I wanted to see Leon and Slim."

"And then, I hope, you are locking the door."

"Yes."

"Good. It's about time, if you ask me."

His Honor, as if in agreement, flew up and landed on Ingelby's shoulder.

"What happened at the inquest?" asked AJ.

"Mrs. Meacock was found guilty of the murder of Samuel Dalton and of William Bramwell. Married to the arsenic bottle was she. Those in high places now agree with Mr. Stone that Annie Sorrell was wrongly hanged, but once a noose has been placed around a person's neck and they have been dropped, nothing can bring them back, innocent or guilty."

"No," said AJ. "Do you know where Slim and Leon might be?"

"I have a good idea," said Ingleby, picking up his hat. "Come. Once more we will go a-wandering, Mr. Jobey, for you will never find them by yourself."

AJ tried to take in every detail, each step, in a farewell to a city he wished he had seen more of. Tucked behind Smithfield Market was an alley that led into a cobbled yard where stood an ancient tavern. Several dandies were leaving, their clothes garish against the gray background, their hats laughably tall.

"Mind your head," said Ingleby, bending to enter.

The place was dark inside, and warm. It was furnished with scrubbed wooden tables, where men sat drinking and talking; a cloud of tobacco smoke hung just below the ceiling.

"Ingleby!" someone called.

"They are through there," said Ingleby. "I will be here, waiting."

AJ nodded.

Leon and Slim were playing cards in the snug near a roaring fire. They stood up and hugged AJ.

"Whoa, look at you, bro. Good to see you better," said Slim.

"It's just great to see you," said AJ and for a moment, one perfect moment, all was as it should be.

The barman brought three tankards of beer. They ordered food and AJ told them how well Esme had taken to the electronic jungle. They talked about Norris and Elsie and her wardrobe. They told each other stories and remembered the good times.

Three plates of steak and kidney pudding were brought to the table.

"I'm famished," said Slim, tucking in.

The three friends ate as they had always done when hungry—in silence.

Leon was the first to push away his empty plate.

"One of the best steak and kidney puddings of any century," he said.

Slim wiped his mouth on a napkin.

"You know that Madeira Mrs. Renwick was sent? Turns out, there was enough arsenic in it to kill half of London."

"They call Mrs. Meacock the Clerkenwell Poisoner," said Leon.

"So it's all sorted," said Slim. "Now you should go back and lock your door."

"No," said AJ. "I'm going to stay with you two, hang out for a few days."

Slim pulled uncomfortably at his collar.

"That's not a good idea," he said. "I told Dora you'd gone abroad and wouldn't be coming back. I can't keep lying to her."

"Wait," said AJ. "Are you really sure you want to stay here?"

"Yes," said Slim. "The minute I met Dora I knew I would stay."

"Bro," said Leon. "We've made up our minds."

There was an awkward silence. The noise of the room flooded in on AJ.

"You see," said Leon at last, "here I mean something. I'm someone, I'm my own man. Finding out about Mad Martha Meacock, putting it all together, was the most interesting thing I've ever done. There are no detectives yet, but I'm sure I can be one—it's what I want to do."

"You know what it means if I say goodbye," said AJ. "It means we'll never see each other again and you can't change your mind. You'll be stuck here forever."

"We know that," said Slim.

"People will be looking for you," said AJ.

"No they won't," said Leon. "I'll be nothing but a forgotten statistic."

AJ turned to Slim. "I saw your uncle," he said, hearing himself sounding more and more desperate. "He wanted to know where you were and said—"

Slim interrupted him. "And said that I would probably end up in prison."

Leon put his hand on AJ's arm. He hadn't realized he was crying.

"Then I'll stay here too," he said, angrily wiping his tears away.

"No," said Leon. "You, my friend, belong in the future, with Esme. That's your time. Our time is here—and for that I thank you."

AJ was so upset and defeated by his friends' decision that

he didn't see Ingleby walk into the snug. He felt a hand on his shoulder.

"Come along," said Ingleby. "Home with you, Mr. Jobey."

AJ stood up. He felt like a little boy being taken away from the party.

"I hate goodbyes," said Slim. "I don't really do them. And I'm not saying goodbye to you. Shall I tell you why?"

AJ nodded.

"Because wherever you are, wherever I am, you are here in my heart, bro, and no one can take that away. Not a door, not a century, not a lifetime."

Leon hugged AJ.

"Without you I would've been completely lost. Now I'm not drifting, I have a purpose. Just get out of here before I turn into a marshmallow and start blubbing. I love you, bro."

AJ couldn't see much as Ingleby guided him out of the tavern.

"Just keep walking," Ingleby said quietly. "Don't turn round. Face the future."

If there was still earth under his feet AJ couldn't feel it as he locked Jobey's door. Some journeys, no matter how short they might be, are harder than others. Never again in AJ's life would he make one as painful as the one he made that night.

He was halfway home before he realized the key was in his pocket.

ACKNOWLEDGMENTS

A huge thank-you to Jacky Bateman for her untiring patience and her inspiration in my foggiest moments. She is a trusted light.

I am grateful to Charles Henty, the Secondary of London, who showed me around the Old Bailey, and to Jeffrey Freeman for introducing me to James Shortall, the senior clerk at 29 Bedford Row. James too ʼme out of his very busy schedule to talk to me and to assure that someone like AJ would stand a chance being given an ʼrview at such prestigious chambers.

Finally, I want to thank a ghost. G e Edinger left me his library and a love of history. He believe ʼ past was alive in the present and the present is all that is at from the past.

ABOUT THE AUTHOR

Sally Gardner is a multi-award-winning novelist whose *Maggot Moon* was a Michael L. Printz Honor Book and in the UK won both the Costa Children's Book Prize and the Carnegie Medal. Gardner's genre-defying novel *The Double Shadow* received great critical acclaim and was long-listed for the Carnegie Medal. *The Red Necklace* (shortlisted for the *Guardian* Book Prize) and *The Silver Blade* are set during the French Revolution; the film rights for both have been purchased by Dominic West. Gardner also won the Nestlé Children's Book Prize for her debut novel, *I, Coriander.* She is the author of the popular middle-grade series Wings & Co. Fairy Detective Agency, hailed as "Agatha Christie for kids." Her most recent young adult novel is *Tinder,* a modern Gothic tale, illustrated by David Roberts.

Visit Sally online at sallygardner.net and follow @TheSallyGardner on Twitter.